P9-EGC-306

The Song of the Winns

❧

The SECRET of the
GINGER MICE

The Song of the Winns

The SECRET *of the* GINGER MICE

·BOOK ONE·

BY FRANCES WATTS
illustrated by David Francis

RP|KIDS
PHILADELPHIA · LONDON

ISBN 978-0-7624-4410-6
Library of Congress Control Number: 2011938796

E-book ISBN 978-0-7624-4513-4

9 8 7 6 5 4 3 2 1
Digit on the right indicates the number of this printing

Cover design by Frances J. Soo Ping Chow
Interior design by Frances J. Soo Ping Chow, based on
the original layout by Ingrid Kwong
Typography: Fairfield, HT Gelateria, Lady Rene, and Perpetua

This edition published by Running Press Kids
An Imprint of Running Press Book Publishers
A Member of the Perseus Books Group
2300 Chestnut Street
Philadelphia, PA 19103–4371

Visit us on the web!
www.runningpress.com

For David, always

Table of Contents

1

Alex, Alice, and Alistair

listair? Alistair!" It was Alice. "Come over here and let me hold you by the tail."

"No way," said Alistair. "I'm busy." He quickly picked up his book.

"Alistair," said his sister impatiently, "why waste your time *reading* about adventures when you could be *having* them? Come on, we need you."

Alistair didn't see how being held by the tail by his sister who was standing on the back of the couch qualified as an adventure, but he got up from his chair and walked over anyway. He would help her in any way that did *not* involve being held by the tail.

His brother, Alex, was lying face down on the couch. It seemed the somersault he'd been attempting had turned into a belly flop.

"You need to spring from the knees more, Alex," Uncle Ebenezer advised. "So anyway, like I was saying earlier, the most difficult kind of somersault to do is when you're holding another mouse by the tail. Why, I remember being up a tree one time when, just as I was reaching for a delicious ripe Camembert, I heard a desperate squeak behind me and turned to see Rebus teetering on the branch." He wobbled wildly on the rug to show them what he meant, waggling his mustache for extra emphasis. "Your father always was a bit clumsy," he remarked.

Uncle Ebenezer had happened to mention during dinner that he had been a particularly excellent somersaulter in his youth. "Not just ordinary somersaults, you understand—*daring, death-defying* somersaults from high places," he'd said.

Now Alice and Alex were keen to test their own somersaulting prowess.

Unlike his brother and sister, Alistair was more interested in the story than the somersaulting, and as he stood beside the couch trying to keep his tail from Alice's grasp, he considered which question he should ask out of the many that had occurred to him. The obvious ones, he knew, would be: Where was the tree and what was the Camembert doing in it? But he also knew that the answer would make no more sense than his uncle's explanation of why the Stilton had been in an underwater cavern or why the hunk of cheddar had been hidden under a bush at the top of a treacherous cliff in other stories Ebenezer had told the triplets. So instead he asked: "What did you do?"

Uncle Ebenezer nodded, as if this was indeed the most appropriate question, and said, "Well, I had to make a quick decision: save my brother, or save the Camembert. Of course, I saved Rebus—though rarely have I encountered such a ripe, runny Camembert." He looked dreamily at the ceiling for a moment, then continued.

"Just as your father toppled forward from the branch I flung myself backward, hooking my knees around the limb, swinging forward—or was it backward?—to grab Rebus by the tail. Then I kept swinging, higher and higher, until I had enough momentum to somersault off the branch and land at the bottom of the tree. Rebus was rather shaken, naturally, so I slung him over my shoulder and carried him home. I have always been extremely agile," he added modestly, raising his eyebrows at his nephews and niece.

"With the truth," muttered Aunt Beezer, who was sitting at the dining table marking essays. She met

Alistair's eye and gave him a wink. Alistair's aunt was a math professor and, unlike her husband, was always extremely accurate.

Alex, Alice, and Alistair had been living with their aunt and uncle in their tiny apartment in the small town of Smiggins for four years now. The triplets had come for a two-week visit while their parents were on what was supposed to be a short business trip, but there had been an accident, and Rebus and Emmeline had never returned.

Four years . . . Alistair's memories of their home in Stubbins were becoming fainter, but sometimes, when he least expected it, he would suddenly remember the sheen of his mother's brown fur as it caught the light from the hall when she came in to kiss him good night. Or the way his father's whiskers creased when he smiled, which he did often.

Alistair tugged idly at the ends of the scarf wrapped around his neck and recalled the night his mother had given it to him.

"Keep it safe," his mother told him as she laid the scarf on Alistair's pillow, "and never lose it."

He had immediately recognized it as the one she had been knitting by the fire night after night in the weeks before she and the triplets' father had gone away. Emmeline was always knitting, and for the first eight

12

years of Alistair's life the sound of her needles clicking was the first thing he heard when he woke up, and the last thing he heard when he went to sleep. She also dyed her own wool in dazzling hues, often with Alistair's help, and knitted everything in vivid stripes—except this scarf. He had watched as the scarf grew, filled with strange shapes and squiggles in every color he had ever seen (like saffron and emerald green and turquoise) and some he hadn't even heard of (like heliotrope and vermilion and ultramarine). There was only one distinct stripe, a blue one, running down the whole length of the scarf. It was a curious creation, unlike anything Emmeline had ever made before, but Alistair thought the scarf was very beautiful. He couldn't believe that all along she had been knitting it for him.

Alistair couldn't explain why, but it seemed to him that his mother's words as she had given him the scarf that last night had carried a special weight. That the scarf represented a special promise between the two of them. He'd even, as time wore on, started to feel that to lose the scarf would be to forget his mother in some way. And so he wore the scarf every day and every night, even when, like now, it was the middle of summer. The only time he took it off was to have a bath or when he went swimming—or when Uncle Ebenezer insisted that he be allowed to wash it once in a while. . . .

Uncle Ebenezer's story about rescuing their father as he fell from the tree branch had inspired Alice and Alex, and they were now hanging upside down by their knees from the back of the couch.

"Like this, Uncle?" said Alice. "It's easy!"

"Not so easy if you are holding another mouse by the tail," Ebenezer pointed out, so that Alex immediately tried to grab at Alice's tail, saying, "Let me try it!" Then Alice succeeded in grabbing Alex's tail, while their uncle was crying above the kerfuffle, "But don't forget the swinging—you have to be swinging as well . . . Come on, Alistair—give it a go!"

All three young mice, urged on by their uncle, had made several noisy attempts to launch themselves off the back of the couch—with no notable success—when Aunt Beezer came to stand over them.

She shook her head, frowning. "You three . . . ," she said.

Thinking that their noise must be disturbing her, Alex, Alice, and Alistair hung their heads guiltily. At least, they would have if their heads hadn't been hanging upside down already. But when Alistair dropped off the couch and was able to see his aunt the right way up he realized she was smiling.

"You three are like chalk and cheese and a ping-pong ball." And indeed, considering they were triplets, they looked nothing alike. Alex was tall, solid, and strong; if he wanted to beat Alice in a fight, he just sat on her. Then again, Alice, though small, was fast and wiry, and was usually able to outrun Alex before he could sit on her. Alistair, who was of average height and build, tried to avoid situations where he might be squashed or chased (which by his reckoning made him the most sensible of the three). Of course, it was not only in size that they differed: Alex was white, like their father, with a patch of brown on his right shoulder blade; Alice was a deep chocolate brown, like their mother, with a white patch on her left hip. Alistair was ginger, like—like no other mouse he had ever seen, though his parents had assured him there were plenty of other ginger mice in the world, just none in Stubbins (or, as it turned out, Smiggins).

"And what's more," said Aunt Beezer, interrupting the beginning of an argument between Alex and Alice over which of them was chalk, which was cheese, and who might be the ping-pong ball, "you're going about that all the wrong way. A couch is *not* a tree branch— you have to adapt your methods accordingly." She sprang lightly onto the back of the sofa then dived off headfirst, doing a somersault in the air before landing gracefully on her feet.

"Wow, Aunt Beezer!" Her nephews, niece, and husband applauded loudly.

"Show *us* how to do that!" cried Alex.

And the rest of the evening until bedtime was spent somersaulting off the back of the couch until they had all mastered the trick (except Uncle Ebenezer, who apparently wasn't as agile as he used to be).

That night, Alistair slipped immediately into a deep and dreamless sleep, until he was woken by a tapping on the shutters shortly after midnight.

Alex yawned and stretched and opened his eyes to the sunlight battering at his eyelids. Someone must have opened the shutters, even though it was only—he glanced at the clock on the bedside table—six thirty. Six thirty! He glanced over at his sister's bed. She was asleep with her head buried under her pillow. Alistair's bed, which was right under the open window, was empty.

With a sigh Alex pulled back the covers. There was no chance he'd get back to sleep now. He might as well see if there was any of last night's cheesecake left over. He padded out to the kitchen, expecting to see his brother there. But Alistair wasn't in the kitchen, or the lounge/dining room, or the bathroom. And as he passed the front door, he noticed that the chain was still on. Alex forgot about food for a moment, and went to listen at his aunt and uncle's bedroom door, but all he could hear was Ebenezer's loud trumpeting snore, punctuated by Beezer's sighing whistle—no Alistair.

Curious now, and a bit worried, he returned to the bedroom. "Alice," he said, shaking his sister, "Alistair's gone."

Alice muttered something and shook him off, but he pulled the pillow from her head and repeated, "Alistair's gone."

"I don't blame him," said Alice, grabbing for her pillow. "If you don't stop shaking me *I'll* leave too. It *is* school holidays, you know. We're allowed to sleep late—or get up early, if you're Alistair."

"I'm serious, sis. I've searched the whole flat, and he's not here."

"So maybe he's outside."

"But the chain is still on the door," Alex said.

"Huh." Alice was silenced for a moment. "That *is* strange." Yawning, she threw back the bed covers and sat on the edge of the bed. "How about the window?"

"Well, I wouldn't risk trying to climb down from the third floor, and if I wouldn't there's no way Alistair would."

They both went to the window and looked out. Below them was a vegetable patch belonging to Mr. Grudge who lived on the first floor, and then a small square of lawn, and beyond that a road which would soon be busy with mice going to work or doing the shopping, but at this hour was still quiet. Even Mr. Grudge, who rose with the sparrows to do the watering before the sun grew too hot, wasn't in his garden.

As Alice craned over the windowsill a flutter of turquoise caught her eye—a piece of wool was snagged on the corner of the half-open shutter.

"Alex," she said, turning to face her brother, "was Alistair wearing his scarf when he went to bed?"

Alex shrugged. "I guess so. He hardly ever takes it off."

"Then I think we can say for sure that Alistair went through this window."

"But how?" demanded Alex. "And why? It doesn't make any sense."

Alice stuck her head out the window again. "Alistair!" she hissed in a loud whisper. "Alistair, are you out there?"

Alex jostled her aside. "Alistair!" he bellowed.

Alice hit him on the arm. "Not so loud—you'll wake Aunt Beezer and Uncle Ebenezer."

"You wouldn't want to do that," said a voice behind them.

Both mice jumped. It was their aunt, her eyes alert though her creamy fur was rumpled. Alice could hear Ebenezer's snores still rumbling faintly from the room next door.

"What is it?" said Beezer. "Is something wrong?" Her gaze darted from her niece to her nephew and back again. "Where's Alistair?"

It seemed to Alice almost as if her aunt was expecting trouble. Her throat was dry suddenly. "He's . . . gone," she said.

Her aunt put a warm hand on Alice's shoulder and, without turning around, called sharply, "Ebenezer? Wake up—Alistair's gone."

At once her uncle's rumbling ceased. "Oh no," they heard him mutter, his voice croaky with sleep. "Oh no . . . " Again it seemed to Alice that while his reaction was immediate, urgent even, he had responded more with dismay than surprise. He shuffled into the triplets' room, indentations from his pillow still visible in his tan fur.

"So you say Alistair has left the apartment through the window?" Beezer began.

"That's right," said Alex, looking perplexed. "The shutters were open and so was the window, and the chain is still on the door."

"And there's a piece of wool from Alistair's scarf caught on the shutter," Alice added.

Ebenezer gently shooed his niece and nephew away from the window and leaned out himself.

"I see. Well, it seems to me there are three

possibilities," Beezer said, ticking them off on her fingers. "One: he's fallen."

Ebenezer, still half out the window, shook his head. "I don't think so. If he'd fallen, we'd see him lying three stories down in the lettuce patch. But there's no sign of him out here."

"Two: he's run away. Maybe with the help of a friend and a ladder?"

Alice shook her head. "Alistair would never run away. He has no reason to. And besides, he would never worry us like that."

"Never," Alex confirmed.

"Then that only leaves the third option," said their aunt. She looked grave. "Alistair has been kidnapped!"

2

༄ ༄

Tibby Rose

Far away, over the mountains and then a sea and then some more mountains, lived a young mouse by the name of Tibby Rose.

How Tibby Rose came to be living with her grandpa and great-aunt in their big old white house on a hill at the edge of Templeton was the most dramatic thing ever to happen in her otherwise utterly undramatic life.

She had arrived nearly twelve years ago. The night was dark and moonless, and very windy. Great-Aunt Harriet particularly remembered the wind, because when she first heard the tapping sound she thought it must be a branch of the giant oak tree at the left side of the house knocking against an upstairs window pane. But no, when the wind dropped for a moment, they both clearly heard that the knocking was coming from the front door.

Grandpa Nelson reached the door first and when he threw it open was overjoyed to see his daughter, Lucia. Two years earlier Lucia had fled the house in the middle of the night to marry a mouse who was "nothing but trouble," according to Great-Aunt Harriet (who had helped raise her niece after Lucia's mother died of pneumonia). And to this day that was all Tibby Rose knew about her father, for Grandpa Nelson and Great-Aunt Harriet refused to talk about him.

"I told her he'd be trouble," was all Great-Aunt Harriet would ever say, to which Grandpa Nelson would respond wistfully, "Ah, but she loved him, Harry."

Despite the harsh words spoken when Lucia had left, there were no cross words now. They kissed her and hugged her and ushered her inside out of the blustery wind, through the dark hall and into the warm kitchen. But when they saw her in the light, Grandpa Nelson and Great-Aunt Harriet each gave a little gasp. Lucia's once-silky fur was now coarse and matted, and her once-bright eyes were dull. Then the bundle in her arms began to squirm and her eyes shone for a moment as she unwrapped a grubby cloth to reveal a baby mouse, no more than a few months old. She was smaller than average, even for a mouse so young, but that wasn't the most unusual thing about her.

"A gingernut," Grandpa Nelson said when he had got over the initial shock. "A little gingernut."

"Strawberry blonde," his sister, Great-Aunt Harriet, corrected sharply. Great-Aunt Harriet was very fond of correcting people.

"She's rose," said the baby's mother softly. "Like the first blush of dawn." And she told her father and aunt that she had named her daughter Tibby, after the great explorer Charlotte Tibby, and Rose, like her pink-tinted ginger fur.

Then Lucia revealed that her husband was dead, and she was home to stay. Of course, they had seen immediately that she was very ill, and though Grandpa Nelson, who was a doctor, took time off from his job at the hospital in order to look after her, within six weeks Lucia too was dead. Great-Aunt Harriet quit her job as the principal of Templeton Green Primary School to look after Tibby Rose, and after Grandpa Nelson had retired from the hospital a few years later, they had both looked after her together, just like they had looked after her mother.

Since her dramatic arrival at the old white house on the hill that windy night, precisely nothing had happened in the life of Tibby Rose. She never went to school, since Great-Aunt Harriet had decided to teach her great-niece herself at home. If she was sick she didn't go to see the doctor in town, for who better to look after her than her very own grandpa, who had been considered one of Templeton's finest doctors? In fact, Tibby Rose never saw any mice other than her great-aunt and grandfather. High on the hill at the edge of the town, there weren't even any neighbors for Tibby Rose to talk to. The only company she had other than her two elderly relatives was to be found in the books of Great-Aunt Harriet's huge library.

When she was younger, Tibby had loved stories, particularly stories full of adventure and excitement, or about families and friendship. But it had been a few years since she had read books like that. The adventure stories just reminded her how dull her own life was, and the books about families and friendship made her feel lonely. The kinds of books Tibby liked now were factual: biographies and geographies and books about how to make and build things—which meant projects to keep her busy and keep loneliness at bay. Her favorite books of all were the books written by Charlotte Tibby herself, documenting her many incredible journeys and the survival skills she'd learned along the way. Tibby Rose wished that one day she would travel the world like the original Tibby, meeting interesting new people and seeing strange and wonderful places. More and more she felt like she was going to suffocate in the old white house on the hill, with only Grandpa Nelson and Great-Aunt Harriet for company. She began to fear her life was just going to go on and on in this way, every day the same, never changing. Until one day—a day that started out just like any other—it *did* change.

Tibby Rose woke up, dressed and made her bed, just like always. She ran down the stairs to breakfast, just like always. She heard Grandpa Nelson and Great-Aunt Harriet arguing about the color of the toast, just like always. She stepped out onto the veranda and walked down the steps to fetch the bottle of milk that had been left by the letterbox, just like always. Only that's when things changed. One minute she was bending over to pick up the milk bottle, the next she was lying flat on her stomach with the breath knocked out of her and something heavy pinning her to the ground.

With a frightened squeak, muffled by grass, she struggled to claw herself out from under the weight on her back. Finally it shifted and she managed to squirm her way clear of what she now saw, to her surprise, was another mouse. He clambered to his feet and Tibby Rose found herself staring at a mouse about her own age and height, with ginger fur and a colorful woolen scarf.

"Who are you? And where did you come from?" asked Tibby Rose, astonished.

"I'm Alistair—and I came from up there I think," said the ginger mouse, pointing at the sky. He sounded equally astonished. "Where have I landed?"

"On me! Tibby Rose. What are you doing here?"

"I don't know," said Alistair. He frowned. "I remember I heard a tapping at the shutters so I opened them, and then I must have banged my head or something, because next thing I knew . . . well, here I am—which is where, by the way?"

"Templeton," said Tibby Rose.

"I've never heard of it," said Alistair. "How could I fall out the window and land somewhere I've never heard of?"

"I don't know," said Tibby Rose. It did seem a peculiar thing. "Where was the window you fell out of?"

"Smiggins," said Alistair.

"I've never heard of *that*," said Tibby Rose. "You'd better come inside and talk to my Grandpa Nelson and Great-Aunt Harriet." And she led him into the big wooden house.

Grandpa Nelson was sitting at the kitchen table watching Great-Aunt Harriet, who was browning some toast under the griller. "Not too brown," he was saying as Tibby Rose and Alistair entered.

"It'll be as brown as I make it," said Great-Aunt Harriet.

Grandpa Nelson looked friendly enough, Alistair decided, with his round ears and round tummy and snow-white fur.

"It's a gingernut," said Grandpa Nelson, sounding shocked. "Another gingernut."

Great-Aunt Harriet, who'd had her back to them, spun around, and for once she agreed with her brother. "It certainly is," she said, staring hard at the ginger mouse. "Who are you? Who is this, Tibby Rose?"

"I'm . . . Alistair," said the ginger mouse a little nervously, for Great-Aunt Harriet, who was tall and thin with steel-gray fur, bristling whiskers, and a sharp, pointy nose, did look rather fierce.

"He fell out his bedroom window in Smiggins and hit his head and then landed on me," explained Tibby Rose.

"A bedroom window?" repeated Grandpa Nelson doubtfully. "In Smiggins? I've never heard of Smiggins. Is it on the other side of Grouch?"

"Grouch?" Alistair repeated in disbelief. "But Grouch is in Souris."

"Of course it's in Souris," said Tibby Rose. "That's where we live."

"Young man," said Great-Aunt Harriet sternly, "exactly where is Smiggins when it's at home?"

"South of Shudders, of course—in Shetlock."

"Shetlock!" hooted Grandpa Nelson. "You must have had some whack on the head, my boy. Why it would take at least a week to get from here to Shetlock—if you were going by the direct route. It's not something you can accomplish by falling out of a window."

"But . . . that can't be," said Alistair. "This . . . this must be a dream. Yes, it's getting dark and misty. I'll wake up in a minute."

"Bother!" came Great-Aunt Harriet's voice through the haze. "The toast."

When the smoke cleared, after much flapping of Great-Aunt Harriet's tea towel, Grandpa Nelson regarded the plate in front of him sadly. "Too brown," he said.

"It's just right," Great-Aunt Harriet told him, her attention back on Alistair. "What on earth is your mother about, letting you wander around alone like this when you're clearly a very confused mouse?"

Alistair returned her gaze with the unhappy look of a mouse who has realized that he isn't dreaming. "My mother . . . ," he began, then stopped. "My mother and father are dead. My brother and sister and I live with Aunt Beezer and Uncle Ebenezer . . . in Smiggins . . . in Shetlock."

Tibby Rose sat on a stool, which was pulled up to the table, and patted the stool beside her. "I think you'd better sit down and have some breakfast," she said.

Alistair nodded gratefully as Great-Aunt Harriet put a plate down in front of him and Grandpa Nelson slid a piece of very dark brown toast onto it. Tibby Rose spread the toast with three different kinds of jam.

Looking at the stripes of raspberry, blueberry, and apricot, Alistair felt momentarily comforted, and when he looked up and saw Tibby Rose smiling kindly at him, he realized there was also something very comforting about meeting another ginger mouse—the only other one he had ever met—even if she was a slightly different shade to him. And lived in another country.

For four slices of toast and two glasses of milk, no disturbing questions were asked and no alarming information was imparted—though Alistair noticed that Great-Aunt Harriet and Grandpa Nelson were exchanging troubled glances, and a couple of times he looked up to see Great-Aunt Harriet staring at him with something like suspicion in her eyes.

Finally, she turned her sharp gaze to her great-niece and said, "Why don't you take Alistair up to the library and show him your map of Souris, Tibby Rose. I'm sure he'll find it edifying."

The two younger mice stood up, and Tibby Rose led Alistair back into the dim hallway. They were almost to the top of the stairs when Great-Aunt Harriet's voice floated up to them.

"The most sensible thing to do—or should I say, the most *law-abiding* thing to do—would be to call the Queen's Guards to come and get him. Isn't that what one is supposed to do in a situation like this?"

Tibby Rose turned to Alistair and, putting a finger to her lips, beckoned him to follow her back down. "Mind the third step," she breathed. "It creaks."

Alistair followed her, stepping where she stepped, until they were standing in the shadowy hall outside the kitchen door. Grandpa Nelson was rinsing the sudsy dishes and handing them to his sister, who was drying them.

"Well now, Harry," Grandpa Nelson was saying. "You know you don't mean that. He must be here for a reason. Besides, contacting the Queen's Guards would only draw unwelcome attention to us—and that's the last thing we want."

"I'll say it's the last thing we want. Having one ginger mouse in our care is dangerous enough, but *two*? I don't know what they're playing at, but I wish they'd leave us out of it." She banged some cutlery into a drawer. "I don't know, Nelson." She sighed. "I know he's only a boy, and he looks harmless enough or I would have sent him packing immediately—but what on earth is he doing here? I certainly don't believe that cockamamy story about falling out of a window in Shetlock and landing in Souris. Do you think he could have been sent by someone?"

"By whom?" said Grandpa Nelson. "And why? He seems as bewildered by his presence here as we are. Maybe he's exactly who he says he is, as strange as his story may seem. We should send a letter to his aunt and uncle telling them where he is, and they can arrange to come and fetch him."

"And if we do that," Great-Aunt Harriet responded immediately, "how do we know the letter will arrive safely? Do they open mail sent between here and Shetlock? Maybe they'd put us under surveillance."

"Oh, I don't know," said Grandpa. "That might be a little far-fetched."

"Well, you'd be a better judge of that than me. You go into town once a week to do the shopping, while I have barely left this house in the last dozen years, as you very well know. So tell me: Have you heard anything on your trips to town? Has there been any news of *that place* lately? Unrest around the border perhaps?"

Grandpa Nelson pulled the plug from the sink and Alistair couldn't hear the old mouse's answer over the sound of water being sucked down the drain.

When the sound stopped Great-Aunt Harriet was talking again: "—hardly be likely to print it in the newspapers, would they? It's what they *don't* put in . . ."

"I suppose I could ask Granville," Grandpa Nelson offered hesitantly. "But how much can I tell him?"

"Nothing!"

"But he was Lucia's godfather. Surely—"

"Tell him nothing," Great-Aunt Harriet repeated. "Just sound him out, see how much he knows."

"And the boy?" asked Grandpa Nelson. "Come on, Harry—we have to help him."

Great-Aunt Harriet flung the sodden tea towel onto the table and stalked toward the kitchen door. "Not if it means putting Tibby Rose in danger," she said fiercely. "Tibby Rose must be protected . . . at any cost. And if contacting the boy's aunt and uncle means attracting attention to Tibby Rose, then we can't do it. We'll just have to keep him here."

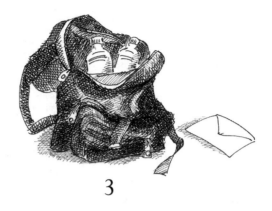

3

Kidnapped

Kidnapped?" said Alex incredulously. "Why would anyone want to kidnap Alistair?"

His aunt and uncle looked at each other. Beezer gave her husband an imperceptible nod.

"I'll explain over breakfast," said Ebenezer. "This is a very serious situation, and one can't deal with serious situations on an empty stomach."

Alex, who hated an empty stomach more than anything, nodded his agreement.

"But—," Alice began.

"He's right, Alice," her aunt said quietly.

Frustrated, Alice took a seat opposite Beezer at the

worn pine table as Alex and Ebenezer moved back and forth to the kitchen, bringing in a plate piled with toast, a bowl of fresh fruit, a box of cereal, and a jug of milk.

When the four of them were sitting around the dining table and had helped themselves to as much (in Alex's case) or as little (in Alice's) as they felt like eating, Alice burst out, "So why do you think Alistair has been kidnapped?"

Uncle Ebenezer cleared his throat. "Well...er... it's possible that Alistair might know something—or someone might *think* he knows something, rather— about...about your parents."

"What's there to know?" said Alice. "Do you think Alistair has been kidnapped by someone who wants to know Mum's knitting patterns?"

Ebenezer's normally merry eyes were somber. "No. No, I'm not suggesting that at all." He sighed and ran a hand over the rumpled fur on his head. "We hadn't intended to have this conversation for a couple of years yet—not till you were a bit older. But as it might have some bearing on your brother's whereabouts, I feel we have no choice but to tell you now, and rely on you to keep what you are about to hear absolutely secret."

He picked up the steaming mug of tea Beezer had placed before him and, despite the heat of the sun streaming through the windows, held it between his hands as if for warmth.

"What do you know about Gerander?" he asked.

His nephew and niece looked at him in surprise.

"Gerander?" said Alice. "It's part of Souris, isn't it?"

Ebenezer smiled sadly. "It's as I thought," he said. "Not that I'm surprised. Of course if Gerander is mentioned at all in schools these days, it's probably only as a province of our larger neighbor to the north."

Alex nodded. "We've learned a lot about Souris at school—Queen Eugenia and all that."

"You might also have learned that Souris is a very rich and powerful country," he suggested, and the two younger mice nodded. "Well, many years ago, this rich and powerful country invaded—"

Beezer made a sound as if she was about to say something, but Ebenezer put up his hand. "It's true, Beezer," he said, "and in the privacy of our own home I can speak the truth aloud . . . Yes, Souris invaded Gerander, a smaller, weaker neighbor, and now that once-proud country is independent no more. Her borders are closed and her citizens are virtually prisoners in their own land, close to starvation and forced to work for the prosperity of Souris. Why, the Gerandans are little better than slaves!"

"Um, this is very interesting, Uncle," said Alice politely, "but what does it have to do with Alistair?"

Ebenezer raised an eyebrow. "What indeed?" he said. "Well, as you know, your father and I were born right here in Shetlock—but our father (that's your grandfather, Raskus) was born in Gerander, and he left just before the borders were closed. And when he died, he begged your father and me to continue trying to free our homeland."

"By yourselves?!" said Alice.

Her uncle chuckled. "No, not by ourselves. You see, our father wasn't the only Gerandan to flee to Shetlock, a neutral country. And many of those that did, and their descendants, like Rebus and me, and good-hearted Shetlockers like your aunt"—he smiled at his wife affectionately—"became part of an underground resistance movement started in Gerander. Its members are working toward a Free and Independent Gerander, or FIG for short. And your parents..." His voice cracked slightly, and he stopped speaking. After a few deep breaths, he went on. "Your parents were not going on a business trip. They were traveling secretly to Gerander on an important mission. But..." He shrugged his shoulders. "They never came back."

"So the accident they were in, that was in Gerander?" exclaimed Alex. "Are you saying they—they were killed?"

"Yes," said Ebenezer seriously. "I'm afraid so. We had

a message from a local FIG contact. Rebus and Emmeline were intercepted shortly after crossing the border into Gerander and . . ." He raised his hands helplessly. "You lost your parents and I lost my brother."

The two younger mice fell silent, trying to absorb the enormity of what they had just learned.

After a minute, Alice spoke up. "And Alistair?" she demanded. "What do you think has happened to him?"

"What is unusual about your brother?" Beezer said.

"How about the fact that he'd rather read a book about an exciting adventure than actually have an exciting adventure in the landfill down the road?" said Alex, rolling his eyes in disbelief. "That's pretty unusual. And I'd say wearing a scarf in the middle of summer was more than just unusual—it's downright weird. Oh! And how about the fact that he actually *volunteers* to help Mr. Grudge with his weeding, and he—"

His sister kicked him under the table. "Alistair's got ginger fur," she said.

Ebenezer nodded. "That's right. And as you might have noticed, there are not a lot of other mice around here with ginger fur. In fact, it's very rare—except in Gerander."

Alice's eyes widened as comprehension dawned. "He's ginger because he's part Gerandan."

"And so are you," her uncle nodded. "And you're not

just *part* Gerandan either. Your mother was actually born in Gerander; she escaped across the border when she was just a few years older than you are now."

The mouths of the two young mice dropped open as they tried to imagine their gentle mother doing something as daring as escaping across a border.

"How come no one else in the family is ginger?" Alice wanted to know.

"It's a recessive gene," her aunt explained. "So a mouse born to one ginger parent and one brown parent will be more likely to have brown fur, because brown fur is the dominant gene."

"That explains why Alistair looks so different, anyway," said Alex. "I didn't like to mention it, but—"

"Didn't like to mention it?" Alice snorted. "You've mentioned it every day of your life!"

"Have I?" Alex looked genuinely puzzled.

His sister crossed her arms and gave him a look. "*Help, help, there's a fire*," she squeaked, in what was clearly meant to be Alex's voice. "*Oh, no there's not—it's only Alistair.*"

Alex reddened. "I'm just joking around," he said lamely.

"But why has no one ever mentioned that Alistair is ginger because he's Gerandan?" Alice wanted to know. "And why haven't *you* ever mentioned it?"

Ebenezer stroked his mustache thoughtfully. "Well, I suppose to most people around here what happened to Gerander is just part of history, and Sourian history at that, nothing to do with Shetlock. They might think Alistair looks funny, but they don't really make the connection to Gerander. Out of sight, out of mind, perhaps."

"Shetlockers don't have much to be proud of when it comes to Gerander," his wife agreed. "We may not have invaded Gerander ourselves, but we didn't do anything to stop Souris. And after the first wave of refugees fled Gerander for Shetlock, our government did close the border at the request of the Sourians."

"All that is necessary for evil to triumph is for good mice to do nothing," said Ebenezer gravely. "As for why I never mentioned Gerander"—his tone hardened— "our family has sacrificed enough in the name of our homeland. I'm done with it."

"But what about Alistair?" said Alice. "If his disappearance has something to do with Gerander, who will help us find him? Should we ask FIG?"

"Forget FIG," said her uncle. "I have." Alice was taken aback by the vehemence in Ebenezer's voice. "After Rebus and Emmeline died I cut off all contact with them. I haven't been in touch with FIG in four years; any messages go straight in the bin unopened."

"But of course we have to do whatever it takes to find Alistair," his wife reminded him gently.

"Alistair . . . ," said Uncle Ebenezer with a sigh, and his mustache drooped sorrowfully. "The question is: Who has taken him—and where?"

Beezer shrugged. "My guess is Sourian agents," she said. "FIG's number-one enemy is Queen Eugenia. In order to maintain control over Gerander, she has to stamp out any resistance. Though I don't know why they'd bother snatching such a young mouse. Really, what danger does he pose? What kind of information is he likely to have?" She shook her head. "I know your mother was very important to FIG—and to the Sourians too. She had some valuable knowledge about Gerander that had been passed down through her family, though what that knowledge related to was a closely guarded secret, too dangerous even to share with us. Certainly too dangerous to share with you children. Unless . . . is it possible she would have shared the secret with Alistair?" She put a hand to her mouth. The next words she spoke were in a low tone. "The Sourians have killed before in their quest to retain control of Gerander."

Alice gave a frightened squeak. "You mean they might be planning to kill Alistair?" Her eyes filled with tears. "But he doesn't know any secret. Why would they think he knows the secret any more than me or Alex?"

"Let's just say the Sourians have a particular hatred of ginger mice," her uncle said curtly.

Alex thumped his fist on the table. "We have to save Alistair," he said. "We have to . . . I don't know." He slumped. "We don't have any idea where they might be taking him."

Beezer tapped her finger on the table while she considered this. "Souris," she said finally. "I think they're trying to keep this quiet—otherwise, why not just barge in here and take him? No, they want to attract as little attention as possible. Trying to get him across the Shetlock-Gerander border would be dicey, as I presume the Shetlock government wouldn't take too kindly to having Sourian agents waltzing on in and kidnapping our citizens. Maybe they'll take him to Grouch, the Sourian capital, or maybe they'll take him to Gerander across their own border."

"It makes sense," said Ebenezer.

"So if they're going to Souris," Alice said slowly, "they'll be heading toward the coast. Which is what we should do." She looked at her brother.

He met her gaze. "As soon as possible," he said.

But their uncle was shaking his head. "No," he said. "Absolutely not. It's too dangerous."

"We can't just do nothing," said Alice fiercely.

"Of course we'll do something," said Ebenezer.

He looked resigned. "I'll call a meeting of local FIG members. There are mice in the organization who have a lot more experience with this kind of thing. *Older* mice."

"Well, what did FIG do to save our parents?" said Alice mutinously. "It's because of FIG that they died, you said so yourself. And how long will it take to get these 'more experienced' mice on the case—while the trail gets colder and Alistair . . ." Her voice grew smaller. "And Alistair gets further away." Then she shook herself and sat up straight. "What time did we go to bed last night?"

"About ten," Beezer replied.

"And it's seven now," said Ebenezer, glancing at the clock sitting on the mantelpiece.

"So whoever has taken Alistair has had up to a nine-hour start." Alex pushed back his chair and stood up. "We have to go, Uncle," he said. "There's no time to lose. Please."

Ebenezer looked at Beezer helplessly. "I promised Rebus and Emmeline I'd look after them," he said. He put a hand over his eyes. "No," he whispered hoarsely. "I'm sorry, but I just can't allow it. That's final."

Beezer rose and moved around the table to stand beside him.

"Your uncle is right," she said, placing a hand on his shoulder. "I know you are brave, resourceful, capable mice, but it's just too dangerous. Besides, there's one question I don't have an answer for," she continued. "And that is: Why now? Why snatch Alistair *now*? Ebenezer, when you meet with FIG ask if they've heard of any unusual activity coming from within Gerander, something to explain all this."

Her husband nodded. "I will. You go to work as usual, Beez—we must act like nothing's amiss."

"Look," Beezer said to her nephew and niece, "I've got another idea. If his captors are planning to smuggle Alistair across the Sourian Sea, they're probably heading for the port of Shambles. It's smaller and not as well patrolled as Shooster, which has a naval base. Now . . ." She went to the bureau and rummaged in the top drawer for a note pad and pen and then brought them back to the table and resumed her seat. "I have some good friends in Shambles who are also members of FIG. I'll send a message asking them to look out for Alistair there. I'll write it while Ebenezer gets ready, and he can give it to someone in FIG to organize delivery." Then she picked up the pen, bent her head over the note pad, and began to write.

Ebenezer stood up. "Right, I'll get myself together then."

As he moved toward the kitchen, Alex and Alice headed to their bedroom.

Alice went and stood by the window while Alex flopped onto his bed and stared at the ceiling.

"I can't believe we just have to sit here and do nothing while Alistair is in danger," he grumbled.

"I know," said Alice. She turned to lean against the windowsill, facing her brother. "They're treating us like we're just a couple of useless kids. I mean sure, we may be kids, but maybe that's a good thing. I think the Sourians would be less likely to notice a couple of kids on their trail; they'd be expecting trained FIG operatives." She paced to the bedroom door then back to the window, feeling so frustrated she could burst.

There was a tap at the door then Ebenezer stuck his head into the room. "I'm off now," he said. "Beezer's already left for work, but she'll try to make it home for lunch. I've left you some sandwiches in case I'm late."

"Thanks, Uncle," Alice said glumly as she and Alex followed him to the front door.

"Try not to worry," Ebenezer told them. "Maybe I'll come back with good news." But his attempt at a reassuring smile was not at all convincing.

"So what do we do now?" Alex asked as the door closed behind their uncle. He went to the lounge room window. "It looks like it's going to be hot today. I bet the other kids are going swimming. It's so boring being stuck inside."

"Don't even think about it. We have to wait here," Alice insisted. "We—" She broke off as a square white envelope on the table caught her eye. The address, written in her aunt's firm, clear hand, read:

Julius and Augustus
Three Sheets Tavern
Shambles

"Alex," she said urgently, "Uncle Ebenezer forgot to take the message for Aunt Beezer's friends in Shambles. Do you think we should go after him? Or . . ." An idea had popped into her head, and she didn't know whether she dared voice it.

Her brother turned to face her and Alice could tell that he'd had the same idea.

"Or we could deliver it ourselves," Alex said.

They stared at each other in silence for a second. Alice's heart was thumping. Could they? Should they?

"You said it yourself, sis," Alex pointed out. "The Sourians would be far less likely to notice us. When you think about it, the FIG agents would be like our decoys." He was sounding excited. "And wouldn't it be so much better to *do* something instead of sitting around twiddling our thumbs waiting for strangers to rescue our brother?"

"I suppose," said Alice cautiously, though she was starting to feel a little excited herself. "But you know, Alex, this isn't an adventure—this is real, and *dangerous*."

"I know that," said her brother dismissively. "But you heard what Aunt Beezer said: we're brave, resourceful and capable. And Alistair needs our help; you know he's not as brave as we are."

Alice thought about their brother, always so thoughtful and considerate and courteous, so anxious not to cause trouble. He was definitely smart, and he might even be resourceful and capable—but he wasn't as brave and daring as she and Alex were. In fact, wherever he was, he was probably terrified . . . And that decided her.

"All right," she said. "Let's do it. But we'd better hurry. Uncle Ebenezer might come back for the letter." She hurried to their bedroom. "What do you think we should take with us?"

"How about this?" said Alex, going immediately to the corner of the room and picking up his rucksack, which hadn't been touched since school had broken for summer several weeks earlier.

"Perfect," said Alice, and Alex emptied the rucksack of schoolbooks. "Wait," she said, as she noticed his geography atlas among the jumble of books. "Shouldn't we take a look at a map so we have some idea of how to get to Shambles?"

She opened the atlas to the map of Shetlock. With Alex looking over her shoulder, she pointed first to Smiggins, then traced the road they would follow. It headed north, through their old home of Stubbins, then veered to the east and curved around a large gray patch on the map before resuming a north-westerly course to reach the coast at Shambles.

"Wouldn't it be quicker if we just cut straight through this gray bit?" Alex wanted to know, indicating the point at which the road veered east. "It looks shorter."

Alice squinted at the small writing. "I don't know. It might be more direct, but it looks like if we go that way we have to cross Mount Sharpnest. It'd be more sensible to stick to the road." She closed the atlas and looked around the room one last time. "I can't believe we were doing somersaults off the couch just last night. It feels like ten years have passed since then." She directed her gaze to the bed where Alistair had been sleeping just a few short hours ago. The sheets had been thrown back, and the pillow was still dented from where his head had lain. She closed her eyes briefly. "Poor Alistair," she said softly. Then she opened her eyes and looked at her brother. "We have to find him."

Alex looked just as determined. "We will," he vowed.

In the kitchen, they found the sandwiches Ebenezer had made for them. While Alice stowed them in the rucksack Alex filled two water bottles. Then Alice took the letter addressed to Julius and Augustus at the Three Sheets Tavern from the dining table and tucked it into the front pocket of the rucksack. "Do you think we should leave a note for Aunt Beezer and Uncle Ebenezer?" She was trying not to think about her aunt and uncle, how worried they'd be when they returned to the empty apartment.

"I suppose we should," said Alex uncomfortably.

Using the same pad and pen Beezer had earlier, Alice wrote: *Gone to find Alistair. Back soon. Love, Alice and Alex.* She knew it was hardly enough to reassure them—but what could she say? Their aunt and uncle, who had looked after them since their parents died, had forbidden them to go, yet they were going anyway.

"Quick," said Alice, feeling a rush of guilt, "before I change my mind."

Alex picked up the rucksack and slung it over one shoulder. "Here we go then," he said, and led the way to the front door.

4

Two Ginger Mice

Just before Great-Aunt Harriet reached the kitchen door, Tibby Rose and Alistair scampered swiftly and silently up the stairs.

Alistair pelted after Tibby along a passageway with doors opening off it, almost skidding on the old wooden floorboards. He could hear Harriet's brisk firm tread coming up the stairs. The curious conversation between the two old mice was replaying in his head. What had Tibby Rose's great-aunt meant by "at any cost"? Not to mention keeping him here. Would he be some kind of prisoner? It all seemed very strange.

Tibby Rose darted through the last door on the right

with Alistair close on her heels.

They were in a neat square room with a large leather sofa to their right, a desk under the window opposite, and floor-to-ceiling bookshelves facing each other against the remaining two walls. There was a stack of books on the desk, and a map pinned to the wall beside the window.

Tibby spun around to face him, hands on her hips. "What are you doing here?" she demanded in a whisper.

"Nothing! I mean, it's exactly as I told you. I—"

"Shhh. Here comes Great-Aunt Harriet. Quick, sit on the sofa." Alistair did as he was told. When her great-aunt entered the room Tibby was standing by the map, pointing to a tiny dot. "Now do you see?" she said loudly. "Grouch is this big red dot here, and Templeton is this tiny dot to the north."

"What, doesn't he know how to read a map?" Great-Aunt Harriet asked. "Don't they teach you anything in Shetlock, young man?"

"No!" squeaked Alistair. "I mean, yes." He tugged at the ends of his scarf.

"Why on earth would you wear a scarf in summer?" Great-Aunt Harriet wanted to know, observing the nervous gesture. "Is that some strange custom of Shetlock?"

"No," said Alistair. He didn't feel that he was obliged

to explain any further.

"Hmph. Well, I must admit it's a nice bit of knitting," she conceded, peering at it more closely. Then she moved her beady gaze to Alistair's face. "Nelson has to go into town," she said. "And when he returns we can talk about what we're going to do with you. In the meantime, try to stay out of trouble." She gave him an assessing look. "And stay away from windows."

"I'd like to show Alistair my treehouse," said Tibby Rose brightly. Before her great-aunt could object, Tibby Rose led Alistair out of the room and down the stairs.

Alistair didn't really feel in the mood for admiring treehouses, but he didn't want to offend Tibby Rose, so he followed her through the dim hallway, across the veranda, and down the front steps. Soon they were standing beneath the canopy of a giant oak tree.

"Here it is," said Tibby Rose.

Alistair looked up and saw a sturdy treehouse built over two levels of branches, with a small wooden ladder connecting the levels.

"Wow," he said, impressed. "That's brilliant. Who built it?"

"I did," said Tibby Rose. "Though I read a book on carpentry first." She pulled on a rope which lowered another, larger ladder to the ground. The two mice clambered up it to sit on the bottom deck of the treehouse, which gave them a good view of the front porch and the road winding down the hill through the gaps in the foliage. Beyond the road, Templeton was spread out before them like a toy town, with neat little buildings and houses, some farms and fields, and a river snaking off into the distance.

"Anyway," Tibby Rose lowered her voice, "this was just an excuse to get away from Great-Aunt Harriet so we could talk. So you really don't know what you're doing here?"

"I haven't got a clue," said Alistair. "I just want to find a way home. Preferably without the help of the Queen's Guards. From the way your grandpa and great-aunt were talking about them, I'm guessing they don't like ginger mice—though I can't see what difference that makes."

"No, that was odd," Tibby Rose agreed. "And what was all that stuff about surveillance—and Grandpa going into town to talk to someone called Granville? I didn't know my mother had a godfather. How come I've never met him?"

"They sound like spies," said Alistair. "Plus there was your great-aunt talking about protecting you at any cost. What was that all about?"

Tibby shrugged. "Beats me. I mean, I suppose they are a bit overprotective. No going into town, no going to school . . ."

Alistair stared at her. "It sounds as if you never leave the house!"

"I don't," said Tibby.

"Are you some kind of prisoner?"

"No! Well, maybe I am, kind of," she said. She looked surprised by the idea. "Though I've never thought about it that way before."

Alistair shook his head. "Look, I think I'd better get out of here," he said. "Your aunt seems very suspicious and I don't want any trouble—I just want to get back to Smiggins."

"No, wait," said Tibby Rose. "Don't leave! Stay for a while. At least until Grandpa Nelson has talked to this Granville." She was almost pleading with him, and Alistair paused. Perhaps he should wait. It seemed so rude just to take off when really, despite Great-Aunt Harriet's gruffness, they had been very kind, sharing their breakfast with him. Then he recalled again that conversation in the kitchen. What *had* Tibby's great-aunt meant about keeping him here? Why? And for how long?

"Please," said Tibby Rose, and Alistair realized from her voice that she was desperately lonely. He felt a twinge of sympathy.

"I'm sorry, Tibby Rose," he said. "But my family will be so worried about me. I really do have to go."

Their whispered conversation was interrupted by Grandpa Nelson calling, "I'm just off into town to do the shopping," and Great-Aunt Harriet calling back, "Mind you're home in time for lunch, Nelson."

The old white mouse opened the screen door and stepped onto the front porch. He had a brown hat in one hand and a walking stick in the other. "Are you up there, Tibby Rose?" he said in the direction of the tree.

"Yes, Grandpa," she said. "I'm showing Alistair my treehouse. See you later."

Grandpa Nelson waved his hat in their direction, then put it on his head and stumped down the steps, along the path snaking across the lawn, and set off down the lane.

"I'm going to follow him," Alistair decided. "There's sure to be someone in town who knows how to get to Shetlock from here."

Tibby looked disappointed.

"I've got an idea," he said. "Why don't you come with me as far as town? Then you can follow your grandpa home again."

Tibby tilted her head to one side, looking uncertain. "I've never been to town before," she said wistfully. Then, in a determined voice: "I'll do it. Maybe I'll get to see my mother's godfather."

The two mice climbed down the ladder and watched from the shadow of the tree until Grandpa Nelson had rounded the first bend in the winding lane, then darted after him.

They stuck close to the bushes by the side of the road, ready to dive into them if Grandpa Nelson should turn around, but they needn't have worried; Grandpa Nelson didn't once look over his shoulder.

"Well, if he is a spy, he's not a very alert one," Alistair commented. "He's about as cautious as Alex and Alice."

"Who are they?" Tibby Rose said.

"My brother and sister," Alistair told her. "In fact, we're triplets."

"Triplets?" said Tibby Rose. "I've never even had a friend, let alone a brother and a sister—I've never had a mother or father for that matter."

"I don't have a mother and father either," Alistair said. "They went on a business trip four years ago and were in an accident. . . ."

By the time they had reached the bottom of the hill, Tibby Rose knew all about the death of the triplets' parents and Uncle Ebenezer and Aunt Beezer and their apartment in Smiggins, and Alistair knew how Tibby Rose got her name (though he'd never heard of the first Tibby, the explorer) and how bored and lonely she felt in the big old white house on the hill with only her grandfather and her great-aunt for company.

At the bottom of the hill, the lane joined a street lined

with single-story gray houses, each with a tidy patch of lawn, flowerbed, and a white picket fence. The only differences between them that Alistair could see were in the colors of the flowers and the numbers on the identical blue letterboxes. The houses looked very stark compared to the soft pinks and pale yellows and mellow ochres of the houses in Smiggins.

There were mice here and there, weeding their immaculate gardens or walking along the footpath with shopping bags, and nearly all of them had a greeting for Dr. Nelson, stumping along steadily a block or so ahead of them.

Tibby Rose's grandfather returned their greetings with a tip of his hat or a wave of his cane, but he didn't stop to talk. He was clearly in a hurry, though his pace was slow.

A few times, Alistair thought he heard whispers and muttered exclamations, but whenever he looked around to see if they were directed at him or Tibby Rose, the other mice were always looking intently at a space just over his shoulder, or at the ground—anywhere *but* at him and Tibby. He felt a strange prickling at the back of his neck.

Soon the houses gave way to shops. Most of these were single-story, but there was a scattering of two- and three-story brick office buildings. Templeton was clearly a more businesslike place than Smiggins, and the footpath became increasingly crowded; Tibby Rose, who was looking a little alarmed by the busyness and bustle, stuck close to his side.

There were mice with briefcases and mice pushing prams, mice on bicycles and mice pushing barrows of fruit and vegetables. Alistair and Tibby Rose were shoved and jostled, and Alistair was taken aback to catch the eye of a thin brown mouse with a thin brown mustache who seemed to be glaring at him. Templeton was certainly an unfriendly place, Alistair thought. The mice of Smiggins always greeted each other when they passed on the street, whether they knew each other or not. Alistair quickly tore his gaze away only to be startled by the giant image of an imperious-looking mouse in purple velvet robes and a diamond-studded tiara painted on the side of the tallest building. Above her was painted an enormous silver and purple flag. This must be Queen Eugenia, he guessed. He had learned about the Sourian queen at school.

It was becoming harder and harder to spot Grandpa Nelson's brown hat bobbing through the crowd, and then Alistair couldn't see him at all.

"We've lost him," said Alistair, but Tibby Rose grabbed his arm. "There!" she said, pointing, and Alistair saw a flash of snow-white fur heading down a smaller street to their left.

"Ginger spies," someone hissed as the young mice weaved through the crowd in pursuit. "The Queen's Guards will get you."

Alistair jumped in fright. Had that been directed at them?

Tibby Rose's grip on his arm tightened. "Did you hear that?" she gasped. Alistair thought her rose-tinged fur looked paler than usual.

"Yes," he said grimly. "I'm starting to see what your grandpa meant by *unwelcome attention.*" It occurred to him that they might actually be in danger here, though for the life of him he couldn't work out why. Because they were ginger? It just didn't make any sense.

They turned the corner and drew to a halt. The street was virtually deserted—and Grandpa Nelson was gone.

"What do you—," Alistair began, but he was cut off by a voice behind him saying, "Well I never. Never in my whole life did I see a ginger mouse, and now I seen two at once. Or is my eyes playing tricks?"

The two young mice turned to see a spotted mouse behind the counter of a newspaper stand rubbing his eyes. He sounded amazed but not hostile, Alistair was pleased to note.

"Nope," he said, when he had opened them again. "That's two ginger mice all right. Now what are you two doing here?"

After an awkward pause, Alistair whispered, "Just follow my lead, okay? And look innocent."

"That shouldn't be too hard," Tibby Rose muttered back. "We *are* innocent, as far as I know."

"Um, good morning, sir," Alistair began politely, moving toward the piles of newspapers stacked in front of the kiosk's counter. There was a paper called the *Templeton Times*, he noticed, and the *Souris Sentinel*.

Looking up, he saw magazine racks on both sides of the kiosk, opening like wings off the counter. These, too, held a range of titles Alistair had never heard of: *Mousewife Weekly* and *Grouch Gardener*. His aunt and uncle read the *Shetlock Times* and the *Smiggins Mail*, but he couldn't see any copies of those here. It dawned on Alistair, staring at the unfamiliar covers, that he really was a long way from home. Indeed, it was as if his home didn't even exist. He felt a moment of panic, but then his eye lighted on a familiar masthead. It was *Gourmet Mouse*—his downstairs neighbor, Mrs. Zetland, had dozens of well-thumbed copies. Feeling calmer, and noticing that both Tibby Rose and the newspaper seller were looking at him curiously, he swallowed and said the first thing that came into his head.

"We were—we were just looking for a white mouse with a brown hat and a walking stick. He . . . dropped something, and . . . we want to give it back."

Tibby Rose nodded innocently. "That's right," she said.

"White mouse, you say? Brown hat, walking stick? Ah, you must mean Dr. Nelson. He just went through there." The spotted mouse indicated a door with the words *Templeton Times* printed on it. "Visiting with his old friend Granville, probably. You know Granville? The newspaper editor?"

Alistair and Tibby Rose shook their heads.

"Huh. I thought everyone knew Granville. Yes, I reckon Granville would be pretty pleased to see old Dr. Nelson. Time was when those two lunched together most every day, back when the doc was still working at the hospital." He put his elbows on the counter and leaned forward confidentially. "'Course, that was a long while ago now. Ten years, eleven, maybe more. We haven't seen that much of Dr. Nelson since his sister got that terrible disease."

"Disease?" said Tibby Rose in surprise.

The newspaper seller inclined his head sorrowfully. "Poor old Miss Harriet," he said. "Why, she was the principal at my school when I was but a little feller— many, many years ago that. She was a tough old mouse; I would have sworn she'd never know a sick day in her life. But ..." He lifted his shoulders, seemingly in acknowledgment of the strange way the world worked. Alistair, who had gone to sleep in one country and woken in another, knew exactly what he meant.

"What—what kind of disease?" Tibby Rose asked faintly. She was gripping Alistair's arm again.

"Oh, awful . . . awful," said the spotted mouse. "Puffed up like a balloon and covered all over in purple spots. And the pain . . . " He paused, then said again: "Awful."

Tibby Rose started to laugh but at a jab in the side from Alistair smothered it into a choking sound that could have been a sob.

"Please excuse my sister," Alistair said to the mouse behind the counter. "She's very soft-hearted. Hates to hear about anyone in pain."

The other mouse nodded approvingly. "And it's a credit to her," he said. "They reckon Miss Harriet caught a strange sickness from her niece. You know—the one what ran away then came back sick? Well, Miss Harriet has not set foot outside that house since the day her niece came home. Didn't even come to that poor girl's burial." He sighed. "It's a sad thing—two good mice like Dr. Nelson and Miss Harriet growing old all alone in that big old house, and her so sick. Everyone in Templeton is mighty cut up about it, I can tell you."

Tibby was gaping at the newspaper seller in astonishment, and Alistair wasn't surprised. Could it really be true that no one in town even knew she existed?

Suddenly a rhythmic stamping filled the air and the spotted mouse straightened. "The Queen's Guards," he muttered, his eyes darting from left to right and then snapping back to Alistair and Tibby Rose in alarm. "You two had better... the Queen's Guards, you know... ginger mice..." As the marching steps grew louder, he cast a desperate look around and then swiftly lifted a hinged section of the counter to reveal a door into the kiosk.

"Quick," he said. "In here."

Without stopping to think, Alistair pushed Tibby Rose ahead of him into the dark space.

The spotted mouse lowered the counter into position just as the footsteps rounded the corner into the laneway, pulling to an abrupt stop in front of him.

"Everything all right then, Watson?" barked a gruff voice.

Through a crack in the slats of the kiosk, Alistair, crouched by the feet of the spotted mouse, could just make out the bottom halves of six white mice in red coats and tall, shiny black boots.

"Fine, sir, fine indeed," replied the newspaper seller cheerily, as though he didn't have two ginger mice hidden under the counter.

Why did they have to be hidden though? Another mystery. But Alistair had seen the scared look on the newspaper seller's face as he had ushered them into his booth; there was no doubt he believed that Alistair and Tibby Rose were in danger.

Alistair tried to make eye contact with Tibby Rose, but she was scribbling on a scrap of paper with a pencil stub she'd found on the floor beside her.

"And what brings the Queen's Guards to my humble kiosk this morning?" the spotted mouse was asking curiously.

Alistair rolled his eyes impatiently. Watson the newspaper seller was clearly a very kind mouse, but did he really have to engage everyone who crossed his path in conversation? Then the younger mouse heard something that made him press his ear to the gap in the slats and listen intently.

"Reports of unrest around the border with—"

As Alistair and Tibby Rose exchanged wide-eyed glances around the legs of Watson, another guard hastily cut off the first guard's sentence.

"No reason," he said sharply, and Alistair saw the heel of one shiny boot coming down on the toe of another. "No reason at all," he repeated over the ensuing yelp.

And with that, six pairs of shiny boots (with one boot limping slightly) turned and marched back down the laneway.

When the sound of heels on pavement had faded,

Watson looked down at the two mice kneeling at his feet with his eyebrows raised questioningly. But when Alistair opened his mouth to explain—though exactly what or how or why he was going to explain he really had no idea—the spotted mouse held up a hand.

"It's probably better if you don't say nothing," he said. "What I don't know can't hurt me." He shook his head and whistled between his teeth. "I reckon you two look mighty young to be wandering the town alone, but I suppose you know what you're doing."

No, thought Alistair. *We have absolutely no idea. I wish we did.*

"And I just don't buy that rubbish about every ginger mouse being our enemy." He stroked his whiskers thoughtfully and then muttered, "Can't say as I'd blame you though, after everything your people have suffered." Just as Alistair was about to ask what he meant, the spotted mouse cleared his throat and said briskly, "Anyway, you came here wanting to do a good turn by old Doc Nelson, so I done a good turn by you." He rubbed his whiskers and added, "What goes around comes around, see?"

As Watson turned his gaze in the direction of the street down which the Queen's Guards had marched, Alistair felt Tibby Rose press the piece of paper she had been writing on into his hand.

Glancing down, he could just make out the words in the dim light: *Dear Grandpa Nelson, I have gone to help Alistair find his way home. Please do not worry about me. I understand now that you were keeping me hidden, though I don't know why. Tell Great-Aunt Harriet I'm sorry, and that I hope she can go out again. Thank you both for looking after me so well. Love, Tibby Rose.*

Alistair looked at Tibby Rose. She nodded, her expression both sad and defiant. Then, as Watson turned his attention back to them, she quickly mimed folding the piece of paper. Alistair did so, and when the newspaper seller said, "So about that thing the doctor dropped?" he held out the folded note and replied, "This fell out of his pocket. Perhaps you could give it to him when he has finished his meeting with Mr. Granville."

Watson took the note and said, "That I can surely do." He lifted the counter. "And you two had better be running along."

As Alistair and Tibby Rose left the shelter of the kiosk Alistair heard him muttering, "Two ginger mice . . . At the same time! . . . Well I never."

5

The Road to Shambles

Alex and Alice hurried down the stairs, eager to be on their way, but when they reached the second floor their path was blocked. It was Mrs. Zetland, still in her dressing gown, her gray fur in disarray. The two mice groaned under their breath. They liked Mrs. Zetland—she enjoyed cooking and almost always had a freshly baked biscuit close to hand—but she did like to talk . . . and talk . . . and talk.

"Good morning, you two," she said. "You're up awfully early for a couple of mice on summer holidays.

In fact, the whole family seems to be. Beezer off to work, and your uncle galloping down these stairs as if his fur was on fire. Though what better time to rise early than in summer? The early mouse gets the cheese, as they say. Not that I'm much of a morning person myself—still, I never say no to a bite of cheese. Now where might you be off to, I wonder . . . and where's that delightful brother of yours?" She looked up the stairs inquiringly.

"Hi, Mrs. Zetland," said Alice. "We're going . . ." She paused, suddenly realizing that she couldn't tell their neighbor the truth.

"To Stubbins," Alex broke in. "To visit some of our old friends there. Alistair went on ahead."

"Really?" Mrs. Zetland raised her eyebrows. "What a shame I didn't see him leave. I would have given him some biscuits for his journey. And how about you two—do you have enough food for the journey? I hope Ebenezer has given you a good lunch; it doesn't do to travel on an empty stomach. But I'm sure he thought of that—that rucksack looks awfully heavy. Though you want to be careful about lifting heavy rucksacks. Why, an old school friend of mine once lifted a heavy rucksack and fell right through the floor. Which was a pity because she lived on the fourth floor and she landed on the breakfast table of the family below. But that wasn't uncommon back when

I was a child. We worked much harder at school than you young mice nowadays. So many books we had to carry . . . And when she got to school she had a buttered crumpet stuck to her bottom. How we laughed!"

"Pardon?" said Alex, who often had trouble following Mrs. Zetland's conversations.

"Some of the food is for Alistair," Alice improvised. "He was in such a hurry to be on his way that he forgot to have breakfast, so we're taking him a picnic breakfast— we're sure to catch up with him along the road."

"Well now, what a thoughtful brother and sister he's got." Mrs. Zetland beamed. "Goodness knows a skinny young thing like him can't afford to be skipping meals. I'll tell you what, I baked a batch of chocolate-chip biscuits just last night. Wait here a minute and I'll give you some for your picnic."

"We're in a bit of a hurry, Mrs.——," Alice began.

"Some biscuits would be lovely," Alex interrupted.

A few minutes later, the two mice were heading down the stairs again, munching on biscuits from the brown paper bag Mrs. Zetland had given them.

As they pushed open the door of the apartment house and started down the path they were assailed by an angry "Oy!" from the direction of the vegetable patch.

"Huh?" said Alex, spraying biscuit crumbs all over Alice, who had been walking in front.

"If you don't mind," said Alice, brushing the crumbs from her shoulders.

"It's Mr. Grudge," said Alex.

Alice sighed. "What have we done now?"

The two mice turned to see grizzled old Mr. Grudge, wearing his gardening hat and gloves, shaking his trowel at them. "You two! What's been going on here? You tell those friends of yours not to walk all over my vegetable patch. The parsley is all ruined."

"Er, what are you talking about, Mr. Grudge?" Alice asked patiently.

"Your friends. Mucking about in my vegetable patch. I won't have it."

"Sorry, Mr. Grudge, but we haven't had any friends over in the last few days."

"Oh really? Then who was that fumbling about with the ladder early this morning trying to get up to your room, eh?"

"A ladder? Up to our room?" Alice poked Alex excitedly. "Um, what did they look like?"

"Well, I can't see in the dark, can I?" grumbled Mr. Grudge. "It was just before dawn. I was up there"—he pointed to his window on the first floor—"and they were down there." He pointed to the squashed parsley at his feet. "I only saw the tops of their heads, didn't I? But I reckon..." He squinted in recollection. "I reckon one was black and one was gray. Anyway, they scattered quick enough when I tapped the window." He pressed his lips together in satisfaction. "If you see them, you tell them they owe me some parsley."

"We will," Alice promised. "As soon as we catch up with them." She poked Alex again and hurried down the path, her brother close behind.

"What was all that about?" Alex wondered as they reached the street. This was the road which would take them out of Smiggins and north toward Stubbins. "And why did you keep poking me?"

"Don't you see?" Alice said. "Those two mice he saw must be the kidnappers! Why else would they be trying to get up to our room with a ladder?"

Alex's eyes widened. "Yeah. And if they were here just before dawn, they must only be a couple of hours ahead of us. Yes!" He punched the air. "Come on, sis. Let's move!"

It was almost noon, and the sun was blazing down on the tops of their heads, when they reached Stubbins. They had been walking for four hours, and Alice was feeling hot and uncomfortable, but she cried out with joy on seeing the familiar silhouette of their old hometown. It had been a long time since they'd last been there. In the early days, when they'd all thought Rebus and Emmeline had simply been delayed and would be returning soon, their aunt and uncle had regularly brought them back to visit their old school friends. But when they'd found out their parents were dead, the triplets had started school in Smiggins, and soon had a whole new gang of friends. They returned to Stubbins less and less frequently, and had more or less forgotten about their old lives.

"Look, there's the park where we used to play after school!" said Alex.

"And the town hall. Remember that Christmas concert where Alistair sang all twenty-seven verses of 'The Shetlock Shepherd' without forgetting a single word?"

"Is that the same concert where you forgot your lines in the play and started to cry?"

"It was a very difficult role," snapped Alice.

"Um, let me see if I can recall your lines," said Alex. "Oh, that's right: *Hee-haw, hee-haw, I am the Christmas donkey*—isn't that how it went?"

"Shut up," said Alice crossly, but Alex was standing stock-still, transfixed, for the cobbled street had opened out into a huge square, bustling with activity.

"The market," he breathed, surveying the rows of colorful stalls. "Quick, sis—this way!" He darted through a crowd of shoppers bearing bags and baskets.

"Ooph," said a mouse carrying a bunch of sunflowers so large he could barely see over them, and "Watch it!" said another carrying an armful of deep purple eggplants.

Alice followed him to a stall where, under a blue and white striped umbrella, a mouse in a brightly patterned apron was arranging plates of cheese.

"Cheese!" Alex crowed.

"Er, yes," said the mouse in the apron, who was clearly not used to customers going into such ecstasies. "It's cheese."

"Look at the mold in that blue," said Alex, pointing excitedly as Alice caught up. "And check out the crumbliness of that cheddar... How long did you age it?" he demanded of the stallholder.

"Three years," said the mouse in the apron promptly. He seemed to have decided that while Alex was clearly a bit deranged, he might turn out to be a good customer. "And for a connoisseur like young sir, I could offer a special price..."

"I'm afraid we don't have any money," said Alice. "We're going this way," she said to her brother, grasping him firmly by the arm and dragging him down a quiet side street and away from the market. Thank goodness he hadn't spotted the cake stall.

"But, sis," Alex complained, "I'm starving."

"Whose fault is that?" Alice shot back. "You ate all our

supplies half an hour after we left Smiggins."

After they had walked for several minutes, with Alice propelling Alex quickly past any particularly appetizing shop window, the shops became houses, and then the houses grew further apart, and they turned right, then left, then right again, their feet knowing exactly where they were going even though neither of them had said a word. Soon they were standing outside a familiar stone cottage with a deep front garden and a small orchard just visible out the back.

"I wonder who lives here now," said Alex.

"I think Uncle Ebenezer said a family with two kids had rented it," Alice said, observing a small bike and a tricycle and a faded pair of toy racing cars on the front porch. "I suppose he was right about it being better for the house to be lived in and loved than standing cold and empty."

"I suppose," Alex echoed.

"Do you think about Mum and Dad much?" Alice asked, her eyes running over the slate-tiled roof and the honey-colored stone before moving to the old rope swing hanging from the chestnut tree in the yard. She, Alex, and Alistair had once played on that rope swing.

"Not anymore," Alex admitted. "I used to think about them all the time, but it's getting harder to remember them. I know that sounds awful, but—well, Aunt Beezer and Uncle Ebenezer are so nice, and I like Smiggins, and our old life in Stubbins seems so far away. I guess Alistair still thinks about them a lot, though—he never takes off that scarf Mum gave him."

"And now Alistair is gone too. . . ."

On this gloomy note, they set off once more on the road to Shambles.

They walked in near silence for several hours. Flat fields of barley and rye stretched to the horizon on either side of the road like a sea of pale gold, rippling with the slightest puff of breeze. The sun beat down relentlessly until the feathery golden grains began to shimmer before their eyes, and they stopped to swig from their water bottles. It seemed that the long straight road would go on forever.

At last the road started to climb steadily, winding through uncultivated stretches of tussocky wild grasses punctuated with tangled shrubs and thickets of twisted trees. The mood of dreariness brought on by the endless ocean of crops now turned almost to dread in this lonely untamed landscape, and the dangers they might face on their long journey north, far from home and loved ones, suddenly seemed very real to Alice. The thought of having to spend the night out here made her heart beat faster, even as weariness slowed her steps. She was relieved when they crested a hill and found themselves in a lush green valley of almond and cherry trees, with olive trees in terraces creeping up the rock faces of the craggy mountain range which encased the valley.

They were walking along the valley floor, their shadows long in the golden light of late afternoon, when Alex's nose started twitching.

"What's that?" he said, almost to himself.

He sniffed again.

"Bread!" he said. "Freshly baked bread!"

As the aroma filled her nostrils, Alice was suddenly aware of how hungry she was.

"It's coming from that farmhouse over there." Alex pointed to a trim weatherboard house at the end of a short lane lined with cherry trees. "Aha! I knew we'd find food when we needed it. Follow me! Farmers' wives love orphans."

He fairly scampered along the lane, Alice following close behind.

The smell of bread warm from the oven grew stronger as they neared the house, and they had just entered the grassy yard when they encountered the farmer's wife. Wearing big black boots and a straw hat, she was repairing a broken section of the fence that ran down to the road.

As the two young mice approached she raised her eyes from her work and said, "What do you two want?"

"Good afternoon, oh kind farmer's wife," said Alex. "We smelled your delicious homemade bread from the road and were wondering if you had any to spare for two young mice with a long journey ahead of them." He turned and gave his sister a broad wink.

The farmer's wife regarded them narrowly from under the brim of her hat. "Are you twins then?"

"No, we're triplets. We got separated from our brother back in Stubbins. Have you seen him? He looks exactly like us except ginger, and he's wearing a scarf."

"Ha! I think if I'd seen a ginger mouse wearing a scarf I'd probably remember it. Do your parents know where you are?" she asked, eyeing their rucksack suspiciously.

Alex nudged Alice and they both opened their eyes very wide. "No, ma'am. You see . . . we're orphans."

If the farmer's wife felt sorry for them, she disguised it well. "So you've lost your mother and your father?"

Alex and Alice nodded sadly.

"And now you've lost your brother?"

They hung their heads so that their whiskers drooped.

"Hmph, it seems to me you are two bad, careless mice to be losing your relations like that. If you want some of my freshly baked bread you're going to have to work for it."

"But . . . but, good farmer's wife . . . "

"I'm not the farmer's wife, you cheeky brat—I'm the farmer. Now do we have a deal?"

Alex sniffed the air longingly, glanced back at Alice, then turned to face the farmer.

"And you can tell your friends there's no point hanging around," she added before he could open his mouth. "I'm not running some kind of free bakery for indigent mice here, you know."

"What friends?"

"Down the lane—a gray mouse and a black one." She waved her hammer toward the junction of lane and road.

But when Alex and Alice turned to look there was no sign of mice of any color.

"They were there before," said the farmer grumpily.

"Was there a ginger mouse with them?"

"Don't you think if I'd seen a ginger mouse I'd have said I'd seen a ginger mouse?" demanded the farmer, her hands on her hips.

"I guess so," Alice murmured.

"Well, you guess right," said the farmer. She put down her hammer, walked over to the side of the house and picked up two yellow buckets. "You see the cherries on the trees over there?" She ducked her chin at a row of cherry trees laden with fruit. "Pick them."

"But—there must be twenty trees there," protested Alex.

"You'll find a ladder over beside the house. If you each fill five buckets, I'll give you a good supper and let you sleep in the barn."

Alex frowned impatiently and Alice knew what he was thinking. They didn't have time to waste picking cherries if they wanted to catch up with Alistair's kidnappers! But the sun was close to setting and they were tired and hungry. Maybe it wasn't such a bad idea to stop here. She poked Alex in the back and said to the farmer, "Thank you. We'd appreciate it."

"Empty your buckets into that crate over there— and no eating the cherries." The farmer gave Alex a particularly meaningful stare. "I'll know if you do." And she picked up her hammer and set to work on the fence once more.

Alex and Alice took the buckets and walked over to the first tree. "Since this was your stupid idea," said Alex, "you take the ladder and go for the high branches—I'll take the ones closer to the ground."

"*My* stupid idea?" said Alice. "You're the one who brought us here. And you're the one who ate all our sandwiches back near Smiggins. *You* can go up the ladder."

"Oh, all right," Alex grumbled, "we'll take it in

turns." He fetched the ladder and began to climb.

They set to work, stretching and picking, stretching and picking, Alex's hollow moans following each rumble of his hollow belly. But as tempting as the sun-warmed fruit was, neither of them dared steal a single cherry. At first, Alex passed the time imagining what the farmer's "good supper" might consist of. "Freshly baked bread . . . a salad of figs and blue cheese . . . a crisp apple and a sharp cheddar . . . strawberries and cream . . . or maybe"—he lifted his half-full bucket to his nose and inhaled the rich cherry aroma—"cherry pie. Mmmmm." After a while, though, he grew too hungry and dispirited even to dream of food and complained about the work instead. "Why are cherries so small?" he asked plaintively. "It takes so many of them to fill a bucket."

Alice, who had barely been listening to her brother as they filled bucket after bucket with fruit, suddenly called up, "It was strange, wasn't it, how the farmer saw a black mouse and a gray mouse, just like Mr. Grudge did?"

"Huh?" Alex stopped mid-complaint and, resting his bucket on a rung of the ladder, rubbed the sweat-soaked fur of his brow. "If she actually saw them," he said. "They weren't there when we looked."

"Well, she doesn't look like the imaginative type to me," said Alice. "But if they were the kidnappers, why didn't they have Alistair with them? And why were they behind us, not ahead of us? It just doesn't make sense."

"I say it's a coincidence," said Alex. "Your turn up the ladder."

They swapped places and continued picking, arms aching from the strain of constant reaching combined with holding the heavy buckets. The sun sank slowly behind the hills, bringing some relief from the relentless glare, and had just dipped over the horizon by the time Alice said, "And that's five." She lowered her last bucket of cherries to her brother, waiting impatiently below. He had tipped his fifth bucket into the crate some time before, and was eagerly anticipating the good supper. "Come on, hurry," he said. "I think I smell onions frying."

"Watch," said Alice, feeling suddenly energetic now that the work was done. She stepped lightly from the ladder to the branch it was leaning on. She sat on the limb, then threw herself backward to hang from her knees and began to swing. Back and forth she went until, at the height of a forward arc, she unhooked her knees and executed a perfect somersault, landing lightly on her feet. "Ta-da!"

"Uncle Ebenezer would be proud, sis," Alex said, picking up the bucket.

Together they walked over to the crate, where the farmer was waiting, a disapproving look on her face. "This is a farm, young lady, not a circus."

"Sorry," said Alice meekly. "Um . . . we've finished."

"Took you long enough," was all the farmer said. "Your supper's over by the barn. I expect you to be gone by morning." She stomped onto the porch and sat on the front step to tug her boots off.

Her two workers walked quickly toward the barn, Alex in the lead.

As he reached the barn, he stopped dead. "A loaf of bread," he said dully. "And a jug of water. That's *all*." He sank to his knees on the grass. "Not even anything to put *on* the bread!" He turned toward the steps just in time to see the farmer disappearing inside. "Call that a good supper?" he shouted as the tantalizing aroma of onions drifted across the yard.

And the two mice settled down for their first supper away from home.

6

Enemies

As they walked slowly down the street away from
the newspaper kiosk, glancing left and right to
make sure they weren't observed, Alistair said
to Tibby Rose in a low voice, "I don't think it's safe for
us to be walking around in open sight like this. We need
to find a quiet place where we won't be disturbed so
we can plan what we're going to do next. Do you know
anywhere?"

"Sorry," Tibby said. "I've lived in Templeton my
whole life, but I don't know my way around at all."
She looked at him unhappily. "Maybe you should go on
without me. I'd probably just slow you down, anyway."

"Look, Tibby," said Alistair, "I'd understand if you wanted to go home. In fact, you probably should. But if you do want to come with me, I could really use your help; I don't know much about Souris—and besides, I'd be glad of the company."

Tibby smiled. "Well, I can definitely help you with that. And as for Souris, I might not have seen much of the country, but I reckon I could draw the map in my sleep." She reflected for a moment and then said, "And I might not know Templeton by foot, but I've had a pretty good view of it from my treehouse." She looked around until a tall round bell tower several hundred meters away caught her eye. "On the other side of that tower is the river. There's a swimming beach near the town, but if we walk downstream a bit we should be able to find a quiet spot."

"Sounds perfect," said Alistair, thinking longingly of the cool river as his neck began to prickle beneath his scarf. Although only late morning, the sun beat down from the cloudless sky so fiercely that the cobbles beneath his feet were glazed with heat.

At that moment a slender white mouse with a folded newspaper in one hand and a briefcase in the other strode briskly around the corner and then stopped dead and stared at Alistair and Tibby Rose in shock.

"Let's get a move on," said Alistair.

They hurried past the white mouse, who watched their progress down the street with open-mouthed disbelief.

Tibby Rose led the way, stopping every now and then as if to consult a map in her mind's eye. For the most part, the streets they went down were deserted; the other mice in town were probably, quite sensibly, avoiding the heat of day, Alistair surmised. In Smiggins, too, they tended to stay indoors during the hottest part of the day, though the heat in his town was less sharp and dry, and the light softer than in Templeton, where the light blazed off the pale-gray stone of the buildings so that it almost hurt his eyes to look at them.

It was a relief when, after endless narrow streets of unrelenting glare, they turned into a shady tree-lined square with a fountain in the middle. Alistair hurried over to bathe his face, then cupped his hands under the water cascading from the upper tier of the fountain into the pool below and drank thirstily.

"Aren't you hot?" he asked Tibby Rose, who stood by watching.

She shrugged. "I'm used to it. Besides, I'm not wearing a woolen scarf."

Alistair gave her a small smile. "Don't you start," he said. "You sound like my sister." At the thought of Alice he felt a pang of sorrow. His family must be awake by now, wondering and worrying. If only he could let them know he was okay.

"Where's the bell tower from here?" he asked Tibby Rose.

She pointed to the far corner of the square. "Right there. That street to the left of it should take us to a path down to the river."

Alistair wiped his damp hands on his fur as they crossed the square, passed through an archway, and left the town behind. The cobbles stopped abruptly and they were descending a dirt path toward a slightly muddy-looking river lined with rushes and large leafy trees. Just ahead of them, water lapped at a stretch of pebbly beach, and Alistair could see half a dozen mice of about his own age splashing in the shallows. Another group was taking it in turns to swing on a rope tied to the bough of an overhanging tree, dropping into the river like stones and then swimming back to shore. They seemed to be having a competition to see who could swing out the farthest.

"Alex and Alice would love that," he said to Tibby Rose. "Hey, we can ask those kids about the quickest way to get to Shetlock."

They continued down the path until they'd reached the edge of the beach, then Alistair called, "Hello? Excuse me?"

A couple of heads turned and a sharp-faced mouse cried, "Look at those two! They're . . . they're ginger!"

At that, every head turned and the cavorting mice stopped their games to stare.

"Enemies!" cried a large square-bodied mouse with a kink in his tail. "Get them!" He picked up a stone and threw it at Tibby Rose and Alistair.

"No," said Alistair, jumping back to dodge the missile and holding up his hands. "Wait! We're not your—"

"Get them!" The cry echoed along the surface of the water, and suddenly all the mice were hurrying out of the water to converge on the beach.

"Run, Tibby!" urged Alistair, pushing Tibby Rose ahead of him along the path downstream.

Tibby didn't need to be told twice, and they fled down the path, jeers and cries following them.

The square-bodied mouse took off in pursuit, pausing only to scoop up a handful of stones. Several of his friends followed, and soon a shower of stones began to rain down behind the fleeing mice.

"Gingers!" cried the sharp-faced mouse, her voice bristling with hatred as she hurled a stone.

"Ouch!" cried Alistair, almost thrown off-balance as it struck him hard on the shoulder.

"Got one!"

Her companions crowed in triumph.

"Are you okay?" Tibby panted, swerving as a stone landed on the path ahead of her.

"Yes," Alistair gasped. "Just keep going!" He could hear the heavy breathing of the pursuing mice, and risking a glance over his shoulder, he saw that they had reached the path. His heart raced in his chest. "They're getting closer!"

The two ginger mice hurtled along the path, ducking and dodging the stones being flung at them.

Tibby Rose was breathing raggedly as the path snaked uphill away from the river.

A hand brushed his tail and for a terrifying instant Alistair thought he was caught.

"C'mon, Tibby," he urged, his own breath catching in his throat, and despite their tiring legs, the two ginger mice put on a burst of speed.

They were running between shoulder-high shrubs now, the path twisting and curving so that they couldn't see more than a few meters ahead. Alistair hoped desperately that the path didn't suddenly stop in a dead end.

As they reached the top of the hill and skidded down the other side, the gang of mice scrambling behind them, he could see that a bit farther ahead the path forked into two. This gave Alistair an idea. In front of him Tibby Rose nearly stumbled as the ground dipped away and Alistair sprinted forward and grabbed her hand.

"Stay close," he said, and as they rounded a corner he pulled her through a dense tangle of leaves and twigs into the cover of a shrub. "Don't make a sound," he hissed in her ear.

They sat in silence, trying to keep their breathing shallow as their pursuers approached. The leaves of the shrub fluttered as they ran past—one, two, three, four, five.

Then they heard a bellow of frustration from the square-shaped mouse who had led the pack as he slowed to a stop at the fork in the path. "Which way did they go? Did anyone see?"

"I think they went left," said one.

"No, right," puffed another.

"Let's split up," suggested the high voice of the sharp-faced mouse. She was obviously enjoying the chase.

There was a pause, then the square-shaped mouse said, "Nah, it's too hot. I need another swim."

The sharp-faced mouse began to protest: "But shouldn't we go get the Queen's Guards? Ginger mice are our enemies—you know that, Snodgrass. They're probably Gerandan rebels."

"Put a sock in it, Janice," said Snodgrass. "They were kids our own age. And look how they ran from us. They weren't exactly dangerous, were they?"

The other mice sniggered, and the group began to

retrace their steps along the path back to the swimming beach. As their voices faded, Alistair and Tibby Rose continued to sit in frozen quiet, despite the twigs scratching their arms and faces. When at last his pulse had slowed, and he couldn't hear a sound other than the distant hum of insects, Alistair stuck his head out of the bush and looked around. "I think it's safe now," he said. He pushed through the leaves and then stuck a hand back into the shrub to haul Tibby Rose out.

"That was scary," he said, brushing leaves and dirt from his fur.

"That was *petrifying*," said Tibby. "And just because we're ginger?" She shook her head in bewilderment.

They set off down the path, taking the fork that led back toward the river.

"I never knew it before, but it looks like I'm the only ginger mouse in Templeton," Tibby continued. "Maybe there's something wrong with me, and that's why Grandpa Nelson and Great-Aunt Harriet kept me hidden all these years." She laughed bitterly. "Or maybe they're ashamed of me."

"I don't know," said Alistair. "They didn't seem that way to me. Maybe they weren't ashamed so much as worried about how others might treat you."

"I suppose there are lots of ginger mice in Smiggins?" Tibby said.

"I'm the only one I've ever seen," said Alistair. "But no one seems to be particularly hostile toward me because of it. They often seem surprised when they first meet me, and I get teased every now and then at school, but no one's ever called me an enemy." He remembered the sneers of sharp-faced Janice and blockish Snodgrass. "What was that about Gerandan rebels?" he asked. "Isn't Gerander part of Souris?"

"It's a province kind of west and south of here. That's all I know about it."

Alistair shook his head slowly. "I don't see what that's got to do with us," he said. They continued down the path without speaking for a few moments, then he added, "But everything about today has been so weird that it wouldn't surprise me to find out that I am a Gerandan rebel."

Tibby started to laugh. "Yeah, and I'm one too."

They were still laughing when the path opened out at the river bank, which was, Alistair was pleased to find, quiet and deserted. The tall reeds lining the banks bent listlessly in the heat, and the only movement came from the dragonflies skimming the surface of the river, which was deep and clear away from the churning of the swimmers. They both bent to drink, then flopped onto the ground, exhausted.

"I still have no idea why I woke up in another country,

and fell from the sky onto the only other ginger mouse I've ever met," said Alistair.

"I can't help you there," said Tibby Rose. "I've gone from being a lonely orphan to a dangerous enemy of my people in the space of a few hours."

"Okay," said Alistair, turning onto his side and propping his head on his elbow, "maybe we should leave the big questions for later and start by trying to solve our immediate problems. We need to work out how to get to Shetlock from here—preferably without drawing any more attention to ourselves. Any ideas?"

Tibby sat up. "Do you remember the map of Souris I showed you in the library?"

"More or less," said Alistair. "Possibly I've forgotten some of the finer details since almost being captured by the Queen's Guards and then chased by a gang of bloodthirsty savages with stones."

"Pass me that stick near your elbow." Tibby took the stick and drew a rough diamond shape in a patch of bare earth between them. "We're here," she said, putting a cross in the middle of the upper half of the diamond. "East of the Cranken Alps, due north of Grouch." She drew a larger cross to represent the Sourian capital. "Between us and Grouch is the Eugenian mountain range." She sketched in some triangles for mountains. "From Grouch, we'd need to travel south to the coast—here." She indicated the bottom tip of the diamond. "It's the closest point to Shetlock."

"So we just head south," said Alistair.

"That's right."

He studied the map for a moment. "Do you know much about those mountains, the Eugenian Range?"

"I think they're pretty rugged," Tibby replied, "going by the contours of the map."

"Is it possible to go around them?"

"Sure. It's longer, though."

"Probably worth it," said Alistair. "We didn't exactly come equipped for mountain climbing. And even if it's not the most direct route, we'd probably save time by being able to travel faster."

"Makes sense to me," said Tibby Rose.

Alistair sighed and tugged the ends of his scarf. "We haven't come equipped for anything," he said. "We've got no food, no money, no friends, no means of transport . . . Are you sure you want to do this, Tibby? Look at what we've had to face so far, and we haven't even left your hometown."

Tibby met his questioning gaze with a resolute look. "What kind of home could Templeton ever be to me if I can't even walk down the street in safety?" she said. "I have to leave."

Alistair nodded. "I'm sure Aunt Beezer and Uncle

Ebenezer will help you once we reach Smiggins. The question is, how do we get there?" Trailing his hand in the cool water of the river he followed the current downstream with his eyes, the steady flow soothing his disordered thoughts. "We should probably avoid towns, travel by night as much as possible . . . Hmm . . . 'You feel mighty free and easy and comfortable on a raft.'"

"What?" asked Tibby, who was idly filling in the rest of her makeshift map.

"Huckleberry Finn," said Alistair. "Tibby, what direction is this river flowing?"

Tibby thought for a minute, studying her map. "South," she said finally. "It starts in the Crankens and flows into Lake Eugenia at the foot of the Eugenians. But what's Huckleberry Finn got to do with it? Isn't that the name of a book? I think I've seen it in Great-Aunt Harriet's library."

"Huck Finn is this white mouse, a kid like us, and he meets up with a black mouse, Jim, who has run away from his owner. He was a slave, just because he has black fur. I never understood how one mouse could make another a slave just because of the color of his fur." He rubbed his shoulder where the stone had struck him and remembered the sharp-faced mouse shouting, *Gingers!* "Anyway, my point is, Huck and Jim travel down this huge river on a raft. It's a pity we don't have one."

They were both silent, the only sound the water lapping gently at the bank, then Tibby said, "You know, I could probably make one."

"You could?" Alistair sat up. "But we don't have any tools or materials."

"Actually, we have got the materials," said Tibby. "There's a grove of bamboo over there—bamboo is the perfect wood for a raft; lightweight, floats well. We can find some vines or creepers to tie the sticks together. As for tools, we can use stones to hack down the bamboo we need."

Alistair looked at Tibby. "That's amazing, Tib. All I did was mention a raft and you work out how to actually make one."

Tibby smiled modestly. "I read about how to make a raft in a book by Charlotte Tibby, the explorer, but I wouldn't have thought of it if you hadn't given me the idea."

"Okay, then—let's get to work. Tell me what I should do."

They both stood and, checking that the coast was still clear, headed toward the bamboo grove Tibby had indicated.

"We need about a dozen bits of bamboo," she decided, "all about the same circumference." She wrapped her hand around a trunk that was twice her height and so thick her fingers only just touched on the other side. "Like this. If you get started on the bamboo, I'll look for something we can fasten them together with."

Alistair found a shallow stretch of the river and began to pick up the flat smooth stones one by one, running his thumb along their sides to test for a thin edge. When at last he had found one that seemed sufficiently thin, he took it over to the bamboo. It was slow hot work, hacking and sawing at the tough, fibrous trunks, and more than once as he felt the woolen scarf prickling at his throat he wished his mother had made him a memento that was a little cooler against his fur. Sunglasses, for example.

He had managed to cut four lengths when he heard Tibby Rose calling to him in a low voice.

"Alistair, over here."

She was on the other side of the clearing, and when Alistair reached her, he found that she had been collecting strands from a thick vine that was draped over a fallen log. This wasn't what she had called him for, though. "Look," she said. "Blackberries."

Alistair had been too preoccupied to notice his hunger, but when he saw the blackberry bushes he was almost overcome by the gnawing sensation in the pit of his stomach. "Brilliant!"

They ate their fill of the tart, juicy berries, then got

back to work. The sun was getting lower in the sky by the time they had a dozen sticks of bamboo, stripped of leaves, ready to fasten with the vines Tibby Rose had gathered. They laid the trunks together on the ground, and Tibby showed Alistair how to loop the vines around and between each stick to hold it firm against its neighbors. When they had fastened the bamboo at four even intervals, they each picked up an end of the raft and carried it to the water's edge.

"Wait a minute," said Tibby Rose as they lowered it into the shallows. "We'll need something to steer with."

She darted back to the bamboo grove and, picking up the stone Alistair had discarded, selected a long piece and began to saw at it. "Steering pole," she said breathlessly when she returned.

Tibby stepped carefully onto the raft, which wobbled a bit, but held her weight. Then Alistair pushed off, wading knee-deep into the river, and climbed aboard.

"We did it!" Tibby cried delightedly as they bobbed lightly on the current. She held the raft steady with the pole planted in the sandy bottom. "Now what, Captain?"

Alistair unwound his scarf and splashed water on his prickly neck as he considered her question.

"It'll be dark soon," he said. "I reckon we pull the raft up onto the bank and try to get some sleep, then head off at first light. What do you think?"

"Aye, aye," said Tibby. "Blackberries for dinner, I assume?"

The prospect wasn't as appealing as it would have been a few hours earlier, but Alistair nodded. "And let's collect some for the journey," he said.

They settled back beside the reeds some minutes later, the raft pulled up on the bank beside them, a neat pile of blackberries in one corner. As he waited for sleep to come, Alistair watched a dozen swallows swooping, silhouetted against the sky in the fading light. He was feeling nervous but optimistic. Tomorrow he would be on his way home.

7

‿ℓℓ

Mount Sharpnest

Alex and Alice set off early, carrying the remainder of the meal given to them by their reluctant host.

"Remind me again how much farmers' wives like orphans," said Alice, stretching to get the knots out of her arms from the fruit-picking and out of her back from the uncomfortable night on the floor of the barn with a sack of grain for a pillow.

"She wasn't a farmer's wife, though," Alex pointed out. "She was a farmer. I never said *farmers* like orphans, did I?"

After walking for a couple of hours they stopped for a

rest by the side of the road, and each had a piece of bread, but at Alice's insistence made sure to be sparing with it in case they hadn't found more food by dinnertime.

The road ahead of them snaked off to the east, while a narrow dirt path headed due north.

"That must be the shortcut over Mount Sharpnest," said Alice, pointing.

"Great, let's go that way," said her brother promptly.

Alice hesitated. "But didn't we agree it would be more sensible to go by road?"

"Sensible!" scoffed Alex. "We don't need sensible—we need speed! I bet the kidnappers go by road, right? So we take this shortcut over the mountains and come out in front of them."

"That does sound like a good plan," Alice conceded. "You carry the rucksack."

They turned onto the narrow path, which wound between straggly, unkempt bushes and twisted rough-barked trees. Huge rocks jutted into the sky above them like enormous tombstones. Some small hardy shrubs and dry grasses clung stubbornly to the steep sides, but the higher reaches were bare, exposing steep crevasses and sheer drops. One lone mountain with a snowy peak towered above the rest, piercing the sky like a claw: Mount Sharpnest.

They trudged for hours, barely speaking, up and up

and up until the sun was sinking in the sky. Alice, whose steps had become slower and heavier as the hills had grown steeper, declared: "I'm exhausted. I think we should try to find somewhere to stop for the night."

"Stop? We don't have time to stop," replied Alex, though he was puffing slightly.

"Well, presumably the kidnappers will need to rest too," Alice reasoned. "And they've got Alistair with them, maybe tied up, so that would slow them down as well."

"Oh, all right," said Alex. "How about we go as far as that cave up there?" He pointed to an opening in the rock face at the top of the next hill. "That'll give us shelter and a good view of the valley."

"It'd be nice if it gave us a feather pillow," muttered Alice. "I don't know . . . What if there's something in there?"

"Like what?"

"Snakes. Spiders." She shivered.

Alex rolled his eyes. "Or scaredy-mice," he said. "Come on. I'll check it out first."

They walked on, and though Alice was sure her legs wouldn't be able to carry her up yet another hill, the thought that every step forward was one step closer to Alistair spurred her on. When they reached the cave at last, Alex went in first, as promised, and although it was dank and dark, it was also silent and completely free of snakes and spiders. So they sat inside the entrance of the cave and looked over the valley as they ate an unsatisfactory dinner of dry bread, then they lay down.

"Do you think we'll find Alistair tomorrow?" Alice murmured sleepily after a few minutes, shifting to find a comfortable position on the stony ground.

But her brother was already asleep.

The two young mice slumbered undisturbed as sunset turned to twilight, but as the moon rose, the cave was suddenly filled with flapping and beating and hundreds of shrill cries.

"Eeek!" cried Alice in terror, covering her head with her arms. "Bats! Alex, wake up! Help!"

"I'm awake," came Alex's muffled voice, almost indistinguishable above the shrieks of the bats. "Run, sis—yikes!" He ducked as a wing brushed his neck. "Stay down."

They wriggled forward on their bellies, trying to avoid the mass of dark shapes surging toward the night sky.

As they reached the mouth the cave Alice dived forward, only to find her progress arrested by Alex's hand grabbing her tail. "Alex, let go," she began, turning to scold him, but in the dim light she saw that he had his finger to his lips. Then he let go of her tail and pointed down the path they had climbed earlier. There, bathed in moonlight, were two mice—one silvery gray, the other coal black.

Alice and Alex shrank into the shadows at the side of the cave as the pair drew closer.

"If we hadn't stopped for a meal in that last town there'd be no need for this ridiculous shortcut," said the black mouse. His voice carried clearly in the still night air.

"I was hungry," argued the gray mouse. "I can't be expected to undertake active duties on an empty stomach."

"Tell that to the boss," said the black mouse gloomily.

"Oh, Horace, don't be such a worry-whiskers," said the silvery gray mouse with a peal of laughter. "Besides, you must admit that goat's cheese omelet was delicious—very piquant goat's cheese that."

Alex suppressed a moan at the mention of goat's cheese.

"It was all right, I suppose," said the mouse called Horace. "But now we've lost sight of them."

"Calm down, Horace, dear," said the gray mouse. "We're trailing a couple of kids, for goodness' sake— they're hardly likely to outrun us, are they? Anyway, they'll be going the long way by road, so we'll cut across the mountains and pop out ahead of them.

You watch—we'll be sitting around for ages waiting for them to catch up."

"We'll see," said gloomy Horace, clearly unconvinced. "Anyway, Sophia, I'm not so sure crossing the Mount Sharpnest pass is really the most sensible route."

Alice elbowed her brother and breathed, "See?"

"Don't be so nervous all the time, Horace," Sophia advised. "It's bad for your digestion. Now let's find somewhere to sleep till the sun comes up so we can see this path properly. There—aren't I being sensible?" She scanned the moonlit landscape. "I think there's a cave up there."

Alice had to stifle a scream. The gray mouse was pointing right at them!

Alex grabbed his sister by the arm, and the pair shuffled silently backward, deeper into the cave.

They could no longer see the other mice, but the voices were getting closer.

"No way," said Horace. "Look at those bats circling around."

"They won't hurt you," Sophia assured him.

"No," repeated Horace firmly. "Not the cave."

"Oh, all right . . . Well, how about that outcrop of rocks farther on? It looks like there might be a bit of tufty grass up there we can lie on."

"Better," said the black mouse. His voice was so close

now that they must be right outside the cave.

Alex and Alice lay still, huddled against the damp cold stone, hardly daring to breathe.

"Are you sure about the cave?" Sophia asked, and suddenly the two young mice saw her silhouette in the cave opening.

Alice pressed her face into the cave floor to muffle her frightened squeak.

"Sophia!"

"Just teasing," she said lightly, and they moved on.

Alice and Alex continued to lie on the floor of the cave, trembling, until at last the voices had faded.

Alex sat up. "That was close," he said shakily. "We were almost kidnapped ourselves."

Alice shook her head. "I don't get it," she said. "Who's following who? It sounded to me like they were following us. And if they're the kidnappers, why don't they have Alistair with them?"

"You're right." Alex thought for a moment. "Maybe they're not the kidnappers," he said at last. "Maybe . . . maybe they're on our side. In fact, I thought Sophia sounded rather nice."

"You're just saying that because of the goat's cheese omelet. You can't judge people by your stomach." Alice sighed. "They might be friends or they might be kidnappers or they might be . . ." Her stomach clenched with fear and she felt cold sweat bead on her brow. "They might be . . ." She swallowed. "They might be murderers. What if they've killed Alistair and now they're coming after us?"

Alex gave a scornful laugh. "You've been reading too many of Alistair's adventure stories, sis. Murderers don't stop for goat's cheese omelets."

Alice had to admit that it did sound unlikely, though she supposed that even murderers had to eat. "I don't know who they are or what they want with us," she said. "But I'd like to find out. Let's follow them and see if we can overhear some more."

"Do we have to? I'm tired," Alex grumbled. Then he brightened. "But if they *are* on our side, we'll be eating goat's cheese omelets instead of old bread. You're right, sis. Let's get going."

Alex leading the way, they set off along the path once more. The bright moon shone some much-needed light, but the towering rocks cast strange shadows which would unexpectedly plunge them into darkness. As they climbed higher toward the forbidding peak of Mount Sharpnest, the path fell away steeply beside them. Alice couldn't see how far the drop was, but she felt sure it was farther than a mouse could survive. Oh, *why* had she listened to Alex when he suggested taking the shortcut? She had known in her heart it was the wrong thing to do. Watching her brother's back as he moved steadily up ahead of her, never seeming to falter or stumble, she felt a surge of resentment. It was all right for him—he was strong enough to walk forever. But she was tired . . . so tired . . . ouch! Alice gave a squeak of pain as she stepped on a sharp stone. If taking the Mount Sharpnest shortcut was a stupid idea, it wasn't half as stupid as undertaking the most treacherous part of the climb *in the dark*. And that particular stupid idea, she had to admit, was her own. Yet what choice did they have? If Horace and Sophia were the kidnappers—but how could they be? They didn't have Alistair. Ouch! As another stone lodged in the soft part of her foot Alice decided that she had better concentrate on where she was going. One misstep might mean falling to her death, she told herself with a shudder, and one noisy skittering stone might wake the two mice—were they friends or foes?—who were sleeping somewhere close by.

As they drew closer to the outcrop of rocks Sophia had pointed out, Alex slowed and turned to face Alice, his finger to his lips. Alice didn't need reminding of the danger. Her heart was pounding so loudly in her ears, both from fear and exertion, she feared that the sound of her heartbeat alone might give them away.

Slowly, they crept forward. Slowly, slowly. They could hear the breathing of the sleeping mice, but they couldn't see them in the dark. Alice kept one hand on the rock face rearing up beside them, edging forward behind her brother, careful not to make a sound. Then suddenly, Alex jumped backward, bumping into Alice, who was thrown off-balance. Her hands clawed desperately at the earth as she skidded toward the edge but her momentum was too great. Her scream shattered the silence as she fell into the abyss.

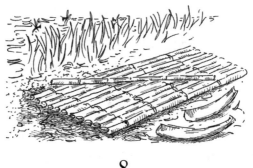

8

The Queen's Guards

As the first rays of light touched the river, Alistair opened his eyes. He was surprised, at first, to feel a stone under his back, a slight pain in his shoulder, the whisper of a breeze ruffling his fur. To see the pale sky instead of the ceiling of Aunt Beezer's study. But as the events of the past twenty-four hours filtered through his mind he sprang to his feet.

There was no sign of Tibby Rose.

"Tibby?" Alistair called in a low voice. "Tibby Rose?"

To his relief, she immediately appeared from behind the bamboo grove. In each hand she held a long thick piece of rounded bark. "Paddles," she said, holding them up.

Not for the first time Alistair reflected on how fortunate he was to have fallen on Tibby Rose, who was proving the ideal companion for his journey. "You really do think of everything," he said.

After an unexciting breakfast of blackberries, they launched the raft as they had practiced the evening before, and soon were in the middle of the river, floating slowly downstream. Tibby stood at the rear of the craft, correcting their course slightly now and then with the aid of the bamboo pole, while Alistair sat at the front and paddled.

At first they passed several clearings similar to the one they had spent the night in, and the odd beach—all deserted at this early hour, thank goodness—but as they left Templeton behind, the shrubs lining the river became more wild and tangled. There was no sign of life other than the silvery shape of fish below the water's surface and birds soaring in the distance.

As the sun crept above the left bank to cast a benign glow on their peaceful progress, Alistair sighed with satisfaction.

"The current's getting stronger," Tibby observed. "We're picking up speed."

Soon they were moving so swiftly there was no need for Alistair to paddle. Instead he scanned the banks to their left and right; he was keen to avoid another close encounter with the ginger-hating mice of Souris.

Fortunately, those mice they did see—strolling along the river bank, weeding small vegetable plots abutting the river, fishing in small dinghies—barely had time to take in the fact that there were two ginger mice sailing toward them on a bamboo raft before they had passed by.

"This really is an excellent way to travel," Alistair remarked.

"At this rate we'll reach Lake Eugenia by nightfall," Tibby agreed.

"Though I guess we'll need to do something about food before then," Alistair said. He'd had a gnawing sensation in his stomach for some time that the odd blackberry from the pile they had amassed the night before wasn't easing. "We don't have that many blackberries left. We probably should have stopped when we saw those vegetable gardens a while back. Maybe we could have offered to help with the work in exchange for some food."

"Sure," said Tibby. "We could have weeded the carrot patch while the gardener ran for the Queen's Guards."

"You're right," said Alistair. "I doubt anyone around here would appreciate our help. And I suppose there's no point stopping at that town up ahead."

They had just swept around a wide lazy curve to see a long straight stretch of river running alongside a town as gray as Templeton had been, other than a distant flash of red. As they grew closer a bell began to toll, and that, combined with the hot sun which was now directly over their heads, put the idea of lunch firmly in Alistair's head. "It must be midday," he said.

"Thirteen, fourteen, fifteen," Tibby counted aloud. "I don't think so."

As the river moved inexorably toward the cluster of gray stone buildings surrounded by a high wall, the flash of red up ahead gradually revealed itself to be a member of the Queen's Guards, standing on a bridge.

"Tibby, look!" Alistair pointed at the red-clad mouse. Did the guards of this town always keep watch on river traffic or was the guard on the lookout for two ginger mice?

As the bell continued to toll, echoing loudly across the river, two columns of mice in red coats and black boots marched through the town gate at double speed. On the beach below the bridge, Alistair could just make out two narrow boats with six pairs of oars apiece. The guard on the bridge was shouting and gesticulating in the direction of the bamboo raft, and it was clear that this was no friendly welcoming party.

Alistair snatched up his paddle. "Help me, Tib," he called.

Tibby Rose pulled the pole onto the raft and grabbed

the other piece of bark, and with Alistair on the left and Tibby on the right they began to paddle.

They sailed under the bridge as the Queen's Guards reached the bank. "You two!" yelled the guard on the bridge. "In the name of Queen Eugenia, I order you to stop! I order you to——" His last order was drowned out by the sound of a splash, and Alistair glanced over his shoulder to see that the first of the two boats had been launched, followed quickly by the second.

"Rowers, stroke!" called the guard in the fore of the boat. "Left, right, left . . . , " he began.

Ignoring the screaming of his arm muscles, Alistair tried to increase his own stroke. "Come on, Tib," he urged, his heart pounding in his ribcage. "As fast as you can."

"There's no way we can outpace them," Tibby gasped.

"Well, I don't like the alternative," Alistair said grimly, putting all his muscle into the effort.

But as hard as they paddled, the pursuing boats grew closer.

"Left, right," boomed the guard, in time to the splash of oars.

"Oh no," Tibby cried. "We'll run aground!" Up ahead, the river widened and the riverbed was visible as the water ran shallow over sandbars separated by narrow channels.

"Take the pole," Alistair instructed. "Use it to keep us off the sandbars. This might work in our favor."

And so it did. Alistair propelled them forward with the paddle, Tibby guided with the pole, and their lightweight raft skimmed through the shallows into deeper water. The Queen's Guards, on the other hand, lost precious time as they ran aground and were forced to climb out and carry their boat through the ankle-deep water, their polished boots slipping on the wet rocks and sinking into the sandy bottom.

"Yes!" Alistair cried. "Now back to the paddle, Tib."

Tibby Rose nimbly pulled up the pole and slid back into her position with the second paddle. They had gained precious time, and they needed it as the river narrowed and started to wind, increasing the strain on their arms as they paddled hard, first on one side of the raft and then the other to avoid crashing into the bank when the river made another of its tortuous bends. A quick glance back told Alistair the lead boat was making up the time it had lost.

"They're gaining on us!" he yelled.

"I don't know how much longer I can keep going," Tibby panted, her face etched with fatigue.

Just as it occurred to Alistair that it was pointless to flee, really, that there was no way two young mice on a homemade raft could outrun the boats of the Queen's Guards, they rounded another sharp bend and his eyes lit on a weeping willow at the river's edge, its long green branches falling to the ground like a curtain. Could they possibly get away with the same trick twice?

"Tibby, head for the bank," he said urgently. "The willow tree." He didn't have the breath to explain any further, but fortunately Tibby seemed to understand the plan, because only a few strokes later the raft shot through the long ribbons of leaves. Tibby flung down her paddle and snatched up the pole, planting it in the sand to bring the raft to a stop. They sat in terrified silence, hardly daring to breathe, as the Queen's Guards came around the bend.

9

~ele

Friend or Foe?

Alice's scream echoed down into the black abyss falling away beneath her feet, but just as she feared she would be swallowed by the gaping black chasm below, her scrabbling hands made contact with a hard surface and she closed her fingers around it. It was the edge of the path. For several long seconds she just hung there, panting, feeling the full weight of her body straining against her tenuous hold. Then she carefully craned her neck to see what was happening above.

In the moonlight, she could make out the silhouettes of Horace and Sophia, standing atop a large boulder which reared up above the path. Alex was standing beneath it, his eyes frantically scanning the spot where his sister had stood only moments before. She wished she could cry out to tell him where she was, but that would only alert the suspicious mice above to their presence. So would any attempt to clamber back onto the path.

"What was that?" Horace asked, his voice quavering.

Alice saw her brother give a start as he realized the voice was coming from directly above him, and then shrink into the shadow of the boulder.

"I don't know," said Sophia sharply. Considering that she had been woken abruptly from her sleep, she sounded very alert. "But something brushed my tail. It was hanging over the edge of the rock there and I distinctly felt something." She peered over the edge of the boulder, but darkness concealed both Alex trembling in the shadows and Alice, hanging from the path's edge.

Her fingertips were aching, and her wrists, and it seemed to her that her grip was weakening. What should she do? She didn't know how much longer she could cling on like this.

"Do you think it might have been a b-b-bat?" Horace wanted to know.

"Maybe," said Sophia. She was squinting down the path now, but was apparently satisfied that there was nothing there, for she turned her gaze to the sky. "Or maybe a bird of prey. An eagle, perhaps."

"A-a-an eagle?" Horace shrieked.

Clearly small matters like birds of prey, with their grasping claws and ferocious beaks that could tear a mouse in two, didn't worry Sophia, because she dismissed the empty sky with a shake of her head and said, "Or perhaps it was a boogedy monster. Come on, Horace, we've hardly slept a wink. I know I don't need my beauty sleep"—she stroked her long whiskers vainly—"but I'd like it all the same." And she lay back down on the boulder.

"A boogedy monster?" said Horace in alarm. "What's a boogedy monster? Sophia, what's a boogedy monster?"

"There, there, Horace, dear. No boogedy monster can hurt you as long as I'm here." Alice thought she heard the silvery mouse chuckling to herself as Horace sank to the ground and curled up beside her.

Alice's arm muscles were screaming with pain now, her fingers numb where they gripped the cold rock. She saw Alex take a tentative step forward, and she followed him with her eyes, willing him to meet her gaze. Wasn't there supposed to be a special bond between triplets? Or maybe that was twins, and the bond was lessened when it was spread over three siblings. She had to admit that neither Alex nor Alistair had ever shown any ability to read her mind at all. Just her luck to have brothers; she was sure a sister would have sensed her despair, her tiring arms, her weakening hold. She would have to cry out. She couldn't hang on any longer....

She had just opened her mouth to call to her brother when she felt strong hands grasp her wrists. It was Alex, silent but with a determined expression on his face, hauling her up to the safety of the path.

Seconds later, Alice lay panting on the ground, concealed from the mice above by the cover of a rock shelf. Weak with relief, she lay motionless for a few minutes, watched by her anxious brother, then she sat up and flexed her wrists and fingers, which were stiff and sore, and attempted to rub feeling back into her arms.

They sat quietly for a long time, listening to the deep breathing above and trying to recover from the shock of Alice's narrow escape. Finally, as the first faint licks of dawn painted the sky, Alex mouthed, "Let's go," and they stood, stretched, and trudged off along the path.

They walked for a couple of hours, long enough to see the dark mountain above turn purple and then a cool dazzling white as the sun eased into the sky. Although they didn't discuss it, Alice felt sure that Alex's thoughts must mirror her own. Whereas they had set off with the intention of following Horace and Sophia in the hope of overhearing something, now her only thought was to push on. By daylight it all seemed very clear. Alistair wasn't with Horace and Sophia so he must be somewhere else—hopefully, that somewhere else wasn't a boat headed for Souris. They needed to get to Shambles and deliver that letter to Beezer's friends in FIG as quickly as possible.

When at last it seemed they must surely have put enough distance between themselves and Horace and Sophia, they stopped for a meager breakfast. As they gnawed discontentedly at the hard crust of bread which was all that was left from the farmer's "good supper," Alice found that hunger was turning her gratitude—her brother had saved her after all—to irritation.

"Thanks for almost killing me, by the way," she snapped.

"What are you talking about?" said Alex belligerently. His ability to withstand hunger cheerfully was virtually nonexistent.

"You pushed me over the edge!"

"I didn't push you, I knocked you. There's a difference, you know. Anyway, I thought her tail was a snake."

"That's ridiculous. Since when do snakes hang from rock ledges?"

"Since when do you know so much about the habits of snakes?"

After this exchange they got to their feet and continued to walk in silence, except for Alice saying, "Brilliant idea, taking the shortcut," as their feet sank into a muddy slush.

"I seem to recall you agreeing that it was a good plan," Alex fired back as the path climbed higher still and the air grew sharp with cold.

Alice, who knew that this was true, decided she had better keep her thoughts to herself. Instead, she focused all her energy on the ridge below Mount Sharpnest; this must be the mountain pass. Once they reached that ridge, it would be all downhill.

When the slush turned to snow some time later, her spirits rose. She had never seen snow before. Scooping up some of the icy white powder, she shaped it into a ball and threw it at her brother, striding along ahead of her. She laughed when it hit him right between the ears.

"Do you mind?" said Alex, brushing the snow from his fur. But he was laughing, and Alice knew she had been forgiven her early fit of temper.

The chill air nipped at their ears and noses, but the sky was a deep blue, the sun surprisingly warm, and as they crested the ridge just below the peak Alice drew in a breath of delight at the white-covered world stretching before them. The path opened out to a wide plateau that fell away in gentle folds. In the far distance, she could see the road they had forsaken, a river, fields, and trees. The ridge itself, she noted, looking to the left away from Mount Sharpnest, was lined with stands of majestic pine trees, their sharp fresh scent filling the air. And beneath the nearest stand of trees was a house. It was no wonder she hadn't seen it at first. A small neat wooden cottage, it was the same color as the tree trunks, and seemed almost to melt into them. By the steps leading up to the small front porch was a sled, and a woodpile stood beneath a window from which a yellow light flickered.

"Look, Alex." She nudged her brother. "I think a woodcutter must live there."

Alex, who had been gazing at the forbidding facets of Shetlock's highest peak, rising to their right, turned and followed her pointing finger.

"What do you think woodcutters eat?" he asked immediately. Without waiting for an answer, he set off toward the house, wading awkwardly through snow that came almost to his knees.

"Hey," Alice called. She scrambled after him.

When she caught up, Alex was peering into a barrel beside the woodpile. "Empty," he said crossly. Then he clambered onto the woodpile to peep in the window.

"Fondue," he said in wonder and envy. "Cheese fondue."

"Let me see." Alice scrabbled onto the woodpile.

Inside the cottage was a gray-white mouse with thick coarse fur. He was sitting in a deep, sagging green armchair before a blazing fire. Bubbling away over the fire was a pot of melted cheese. As Alice watched, the mouse tore a piece of bread from the loaf beside him, stuck it on the end of a long fork, swirled it through the thick cheesy goo then lifted it, long strings trailing, to his mouth. Occasionally he followed up with a pickled onion.

They were so engrossed in this scene—with Alex speculating on what kind of cheese the grizzled mouse might be using—that the voices of Horace and Sophia came as a shock.

"Quick, into the barrel," Alice hissed, and the two young mice jumped straight from the woodpile into the barrel a split second before Horace and Sophia crested the ridge.

Sophia's musical voice rang loudly in the clear, cool air. "Horace, look!" she was saying. "A cottage. I wonder what kind of mountain delicacies we might find there?"

"Looks like it belongs to a woodcutter," came Horace's doleful voice. "See the axes and saws?"

"Even woodcutters have to eat, Horace. Let's take a peek."

Peering over the lip of the barrel, Alice saw Sophia skip nimbly to the top of the woodpile right beside them.

She quickly ducked her head.

"Fondue!" the silvery mouse exclaimed. "Come on, Horace, time to make a new friend."

She leaped off the woodpile and Alice raised her head again in time to see the slender silver-gray mouse and her coal-black companion climb the stairs to the front door of the cottage.

"So sorry to bother you," Sophia was saying. "We're weary travelers, journeying in search of . . ."

The rest of the sentence was lost as the two weary travelers entered the cottage.

"What's happening now?" came Alex's voice from the bottom of the barrel.

"They've gone inside," Alice said. "We should watch them. We might learn something."

They pulled themselves out of the barrel and climbed back to the top of the woodpile. Pressing their noses to the window they saw that inside the cozy cottage the woodcutter had pulled two stools close to the fire and fetched two additional forks. With a courteous gesture he gave up the armchair to Sophia, who sank into it gracefully. The silver-gray mouse then managed to keep up an animated conversation, complete with pickled-onion full stops, while deftly twirling her fork in the fondue pot and managing to tuck away a surprising amount of bread and melted cheese.

Horace, on the other hand, seemed to speak very little, with the fondue requiring all his concentration. Despite his efforts, though, he proved to be less adept than his partner, and was soon festooned with strings of cheese stretching from ear to ear and tangled in his whiskers.

At last it seemed they had eaten their fill, for Sophia placed her fork on the hearth and patted her stomach contentedly.

Head cocked to one side, she listened to something the woodcutter was saying, then jumped to her feet, a look of rapture on her face.

"I wonder what that's about?" Alice mused. Then she shook her head. "I don't know that we've learned anything after all. Why don't we go and hide in the trees where the path picks up again over there, and then we can follow them like we'd planned."

"I'll tell you what I've learned," Alex griped as the cottage door swung open. "We should have just marched up to the door and demanded some fondue while we had the chance instead of skulking outside the window."

"—just on the other side of this woodpile," the woodcutter was saying in a gruff voice.

"They're coming this way," Alice gasped. "Quick— into the barrel again."

Back into the barrel they jumped, as Sophia said, "And

how long do you age it for, Mr. Macduff?"

"As long as it takes," the woodcutter replied. "Two years. Five years. Ten. The longer you age it, the harder the cheese, of course."

"Cheese?" Alex whispered, his ears pricking up.

"I don't know that it's all that interesting to look at, Miss Sophia, but if you really want to see you're welcome."

"Your cellar sounds like a veritable treasure-trove," Sophia declared. "Lay on, Macduff."

The two mice heard the sound of a door creaking open and Horace saying anxiously, "Your cellar looks very dark, Mr. Macduff."

"Cheese don't have much use for light," the woodcutter responded.

Alex moaned softly beside Alice. "You mean we've been sitting in a barrel when there's a whole cellar full of cheese just meters away?"

"Oh, can you smell that?" Sophia said. "What a wonderful aroma."

"Ah, that's my Parmesan you can smell there, Miss Sophia," said Macduff. From the barrel, Alice could hear the clomping of his feet on the stairs leading down to the cellar, followed by Sophia's quick light steps. "You do have a good nose. You might detect an undertone of mushroom?"

Sophia's voice floated up clearly. "I do, Macduff. I do indeed." Then she called impatiently, "Come on, Horace."

"I'll wait here," Horace called, from somewhere very close to the barrel. "Cellars," he said to himself. "Ugh. Nasty dark cold places. Like caves. Could be bats down there for all I know." And on this gloomy thought he leaned on the barrel in which Alice and Alex were hiding.

The barrel wobbled dangerously, flinging Alice and Alex from side to side, before tipping over and half spilling the two young mice from their hiding place. Alice looked up to meet Horace's shocked gaze.

Horace squeaked, "Sophia! Sophia, it's them! They're here!"

But Alice didn't hear Sophia's reply because suddenly they were rolling.

"Hang on, sis!" Alex cried. "We're headed down the mountain!"

And so they were, Alice noted dizzily, as through the barrel's opening she saw a blur of sky, trees, snow, sky, trees, snow flashing by.

Faster and faster they rolled, until the barrel was hurtling at such a speed that Alice closed her eyes and huddled as far down into the barrel as she could, too scared to watch.

Alex, who seemed to think this was all a thrilling

adventure, whooped, "We're heading for a dip!"

Suddenly they were flying through the air, still turning, before landing with a jarring crash that sent pain through every bone in Alice's body.

"Make it stop," she whimpered.

"No can do, sis," cried Alex. "Not at this speed! Whoops—black ice."

He had no sooner spoken than the barrel stopped rolling and began to slide. Opening her eyes, Alice saw that they were now careening headfirst down the mountain. To her dismay, there was no sign of an end to it—just snowy slopes as far as she could see.

"Here comes a bumpy patch!" Alex announced, as their sliding was arrested by a thud. For a moment they were airborne before landing again with a thump. There followed several long minutes—hours it seemed to Alice—in which they bounced and thumped through a field of small hard mounds of snow. When they finally hit a clear stretch Alice was almost relieved as they began to roll once more.

"Woohoo! This is the way to travel!" Alex shouted.

Alice, curled up in the bottom of the barrel, closed her eyes again and waited in misery for the ordeal to end.

After what seemed like a lifetime, the mountain's slope became gentler, the rolling of the barrel slower.

"Oh," said Alex in disappointment. "We're stopping."

Sure enough, the barrel gradually rolled to a halt.

The two mice crawled out of the barrel and stood up on shaky legs. Alice tottered around in the snow, swaying slightly. It felt like the whole world was still turning and she couldn't quite balance or focus.

Then Alex said, "Um, sis . . . , " and the world slipped back into focus with a suddenness that made Alice gasp.

There in front of them was the woodcutter's sled—and on the sled, watching them, were Sophia and Horace.

10

Timmy the Winns

Alistair peered through the curtain of willow, his heart in his mouth, as first one then a second boat of Queen's Guards rowed swiftly past, oblivious to the presence of the fugitives mere meters away. When the last ripples from the boats had disappeared, he let out a huge sigh of relief, then leaped from the raft and pulled it onto the bank beneath the willow's canopy. Looking around, still breathing hard, he saw that they were fully enclosed in a cool green room. As he had hoped, they could look out, while being completely hidden from view.

"A hideout," said Tibby, a bit shakily. "Just what a

couple of dangerous rebels need." She rose and stumbled unsteadily from the raft onto the bank.

They lay on their backs on the soft grass, light filtering gently through the green strands.

"This is getting ridiculous," Alistair said, when he had caught his breath. "We're just too visible—we can barely move without being set upon, and we can't live on blackberries forever."

"You're telling me," said Tibby, holding up her hands, still blackberry-stained from breakfast. "If we don't change our diet soon, I'm probably going to turn permanently purple."

Alistair imagined a purple Tibby Rose and began to laugh—then he sat up suddenly. "Of course! I can't believe I didn't think of it before."

Tibby sat up too. "Um...you're seriously worried about me turning permanently purple?" she said.

"Worried? No! Turning purple is *exactly* what we should do. We can dye ourselves!"

"Uh, Alistair," said Tibby, "you know how much we stand out being ginger...Don't you think purple mice are going to be a little obvious?"

Alistair waved away her concerns. "Of course we'll be obvious—but unless Sourians also consider purple mice to be their enemies, which would be pretty unlucky, we'll just look like a couple of nutcases who've dyed themselves a crazy color. No one will know that we're ginger underneath the dye. And the color will wash out eventually, so we won't be purple forever."

Tibby Rose nodded slowly. "In that case," she said, "it's a fantastic idea! Let's do it." She paused. "Do we know how to make dye from blackberries?" she asked hesitantly.

"You bet we do," said Alistair. "See this?" He unwound his scarf from around his neck and held it out so Tibby could admire the vivid colors. "Mum made all her own dyes—and I helped."

"Well, it's nice to know something's going our way," said Tibby.

With his optimism restored, so was Alistair's energy, and he jumped up and went back to the raft. Carefully gathering the remainder of their blackberries—now a little warm and overripe from their exposure to the midday sun—he piled them into the two cup-like paddles and scooped a handful of water into each.

"Okay," he said, "now we need to squash them and mix them with the water until they're a thick paste."

Tibby copied his actions as he squeezed the blackberries into mush and vigorously mixed the mush with the water. "I'd kind of hoped I wouldn't have to use my arms again for about ten years," she sighed.

After several minutes of squashing and squeezing and

stirring, Alistair decided that their mixtures had the right consistency, and they began to slather the purple paste all over their fur.

"Make sure you get it everywhere," Alistair instructed. "Behind your ears, between your toes—cover every bit of ginger. Here, I'll do your back, then you can do mine."

When they were completely covered in purple goo, Alistair stuck his head through the curtain of green.

"No one about," he said, beckoning to Tibby Rose. "Come on, we need to let the dye dry in the sun."

When the blackberries had baked to a hard crust, Alistair said, "That should do it. Now let's wash this muck off." He waded into the river, shivering at first as the water swirled around his legs in cold eddies. Drawing a deep breath, he steeled himself and dived in. The fresh cool water was a shock, but a reviving one. He forgot his tiredness, his hunger and aching muscles, and remembered instead sunny days in the green glade below the waterfall just south of Smiggins; water fights with his brother and sister, Aunt Beezer's fast neat freestyle and Uncle Ebenezer's ponderous backstroke, his big belly riding high above the water line.

Alistair surfaced, water streaming from his purple-crusted fur, and said, "Wow! How good does that feel?"

To his surprise, Tibby was still standing by the river's edge.

"C'mon, Tib," he said. "It's cold at first but it's beautiful once you're in."

Tibby took a cautious step forward then stopped. "I—I can't swim," she said, looking embarrassed.

Alistair opened his mouth and then closed it again. Of course . . . When would she have had a chance to learn, stuck her whole life in that house on the hill? He felt ashamed of his own insensitivity and it occurred to him how brave Tibby had been, to be facing so many new things all the time without hesitation. Trusting him.

He swam back to the shore. "When we get to Smiggins, I'll teach you to swim," he promised. "But I suppose we'd better start scrubbing."

The two mice stood in the shallows and, with the help of plenty of water and some stones from the river, scraped the blackberry crust from their fur. At last they stood before each other, transformed.

"We look kind of . . . muddy colored," said Tibby Rose dubiously.

"With a definite purple tinge," observed Alistair, inspecting his brownish-purple arms. "But," he added, "we're not ginger—that's the main thing. So, shall we try our luck in town, see if some kind shopkeeper will take pity on a couple of poor purple mice and give us a loaf of bread?"

"Oh, wouldn't that be wonderful?" said Tibby

dreamily, rubbing her stomach. "I've never been so hungry in my life."

Alistair wrapped his scarf around his neck, then they scrambled up the high bank to a dusty road and started walking upriver, back to the town they'd fled barely a couple of hours before with the Queen's Guards in pursuit.

They hadn't seen much of the landscape during their flight downriver, but now Alistair saw that the town they were approaching was surrounded by cornfields, the corn almost at head height. Most fields sported enormous scarecrows—mice made of straw and dressed in old hats and boots. Alistair knew that these were necessary; a crow was as likely to eat the farmer as the corn.

"Alistair," said Tibby, "is that mouse over there green?"

Alistair turned to gaze across the river to where Tibby was pointing. He saw a blue-striped tent, and a mouse tending a cooking pot over a fire. "She does look green," Alistair agreed. "It must be a shadow from the river or the tent or something." He laughed. "Wouldn't it be funny if we started seeing odd-colored mice everywhere, now that we're purple? Then we wouldn't stand out at all!"

They came to a gate in the town's southern wall—glad

to have found a gate other than the one by the bridge where they had been spotted by the guard—and joined a stream of mice hurrying along the cobbled street. To Alistair's surprise, those coming in the other direction were all wearing broad smiles and some, when they saw Alistair and Tibby Rose, even broke into peals of laughter. At first Alistair thought it must be their purple-tinged fur that had caused the mice to smile, but then they turned a corner and saw the reason for the mirth.

They found themselves in the middle of a compact square surrounded by shops and open-air cafés. In the square's center was a fountain—Alistair recognized the imperious countenance of the statue that stood atop the fountain as that of Queen Eugenia. Sourians must certainly love their queen, Alistair thought. That, or the Queen loved to see images of herself. But it was not the statue of the Queen that had drawn the eye of the crowd in the square, though Alistair couldn't see what it was. "Let's take a look," he said, and he and Tibby Rose squeezed their way to the front of the crowd.

What they saw was a group of five mice quite unlike any mice Alistair had ever seen before. The smallest of the group was very young, no more than five or six— and bright orange. There was a pair who looked to be a couple of years younger than himself; one was scarlet and the other lime green, and they were juggling a random assortment of objects—an apple, an egg, and a lemon for one, a tennis ball, a radish, and a potato for the other.

Watching over the younger three were a portly canary yellow mouse with a piano accordion slung around his neck, and . . . Alistair found himself looking into the amused eyes of a very striking mouse indeed. Tall and slim, his fur was a deep midnight blue—all except his left arm and right leg, which were colors Alistair had seen on mice before, but never in such a jumble. There was brown and white and black and gray and . . . yes, even a flash of ginger. A gold earring glinted in each ear. His companions might have been as vivid as the jungle parrots Alistair had seen in books, but it was this dark compelling mouse who really drew the eye.

Yet despite his unusual appearance, something about the ironic gleam in the mouse's dark eyes told Alistair that he was perfectly well aware of the odd picture he made, but that it suited his purpose—whatever that might be.

Then the canary yellow mouse said, "Oy, Tim, how about a song?" and the midnight blue mouse turned away. He whispered something in the yellow mouse's ear, then picked up a fiddle and, turning back to face the crowd, began to play.

Alistair looked at Tibby Rose to see what she was making of the strange scene, and saw her face had lit up at the sound of the music. Glancing around, he saw similar expressions on the faces of all the mice in the crowd, and many had begun to sway. Then he noticed that his own foot was tapping and, as one, the whole crowd began to dance. Dipping and twirling, spinning and jigging, the music of the fiddle flew around and between the dancers, faster and faster, lifting feet and tails and arms into spontaneous movements. Alistair found himself swept into the stream of dancers, feeling a joy he hadn't felt since—he couldn't remember when. Perhaps since he was a small mouse living in a large stone house in Stubbins with his mother and father and brother and sister and not a care in the world.

He danced and danced and, just when he felt his feet could no longer carry him, the fiddle slowed and gradually stopped. The feet of the dancers slowed and stopped too and, as if waking from a dream, the dancers blinked and looked around them. Then, with dazed but happy smiles, they started to drift from the square, back to whatever it was they were supposed to be doing. The small orange mouse was darting through the crowd holding a battered top hat, and Alistair could hear the clink of coins being dropped into it.

"Sorry," Alistair said as the orange mouse approached him and Tibby Rose, hat extended. "We don't have any money."

The orange mouse didn't say anything, but gave Alistair a bright smile as if to let him know that it was okay.

Soon the crowd around the fountain had dispersed, leaving only Alistair and Tibby Rose, and the five colored mice.

The midnight blue mouse, who seemed to be the leader of the group, was gazing into the top hat, raking his fingers through the coins. "Not bad, Pip, not bad," he murmured to the orange mouse. Then he lifted his piercing gaze to Alistair and Tibby Rose.

"So, little brother, little sister," he said. "Did you fall into a blackberry bush by any chance?"

Alistair started. Was their disguise that transparent?

"Don't worry," said the midnight blue mouse. "No one would know but those who know." He winked. "Well, if you are going to join us for a bite of supper"—he paused and raised an interrogative eyebrow— "introductions are probably in order. I'm Timmy the Winns. This here is Griff . . ." He clapped the yellow mouse on the shoulder. "Lilith and Fergus . . ." Pointing to the scarlet mouse then the green. "And this young lad is Pip." He laid a hand on the head of the small orange mouse. "And you would be?"

With a quick glance at Tibby Rose, Alistair said, "I'm Huck, and this is my friend . . . ah . . . Jim."

"Huck, eh?" said Timmy the Winns, gazing at Alistair

speculatively. "Short for Huckleberry, I presume...
Well, the 'berry' part suits, I suppose. And Jim..."
He turned to Tibby, who did her best to meet his stare,
though she was darting inquisitive little looks at Alistair
from the corner of her eye.

Then suddenly Timmy threw back his head and
laughed. "I bet you're pretty handy with a raft, too,
aren't you, Huck?"

Alistair and Tibby Rose stared at him open-mouthed.
He must be referring to the story of Huckleberry Finn—
surely he hadn't seen... didn't recognize...?

But if he did, he said no more about it. He put one
arm around Alistair's shoulders and another around
Tibby Rose, and said, "Well, Huck, Jim, it's a motto
of mine that a stranger's just a friend you haven't met.
So come and join us around our campfire. I'm betting
Maggie has a fine stew bubbling away, and you two look
like a feed wouldn't go amiss."

There was something calm and good-humored about
Timmy the Winns that put Alistair at ease. Besides,
when Timmy had mentioned the stew it had almost
made Alistair faint with hunger.

"That's very kind of you," he said. "We are rather
hungry, aren't we, Tib—Jim?"

"Yes," said Tibby Rose firmly. "*Very* hungry. Is that
your camp across the river and downstream?"

"That's us all right," said Griff comfortably, falling into step beside them as the three younger mice scampered ahead, with Fergus bearing a sack into which they'd packed the items they'd been juggling, and Lilith carrying Timmy the Winns' fiddle. Griff himself held his accordion in one hand and the hat full of coins in the other.

"Where are you from?" asked Alistair curiously.

Timmy the Winns shrugged. "Where are we, Griff?"

The canary yellow mouse looked around. They had crossed the square and turned into a street of shops. He pointed to a dark green awning with the words PAMPLEMOUSE BAKERY stenciled in white cursive. "We're either in Pamplemouse, or the baker is named Pamplemouse. Never mind which, let's get some bread."

"You're the man with the hat," said Timmy the Winns, and Griff, holding the top hat filled with coins, pushed open the door of the shop, accompanied by the tinkling of a bell.

"So," said Timmy the Winns as he and Alistair and Tibby Rose stood waiting on the street outside, "today we're from Pamplemouse." Then he added, not unkindly, "Never ask a question you're not prepared to answer yourself. Got it, little brother?"

Alistair nodded. It was like something his mother used to say when Alistair asked too many questions: *Ask me no questions, I'll tell you no lies.*

The mice of Pamplemouse—though it did seem more like the name of a baker than a town, Alistair thought—slowed to stare at the tall midnight blue mouse standing with two who were muddy purple. But if any of them met Alistair's eyes, they merely smiled and nodded good evening, or occasionally giggled, which was preferable to them hurling abuse and stones.

Griff emerged from the bakery with three long, thin loaves of bread tucked under his arm, and they set off again.

As they neared the camp Tibby Rose and Alistair had seen earlier, they were drawn on by a rich aroma of herbs.

"Smells like Mags has been exercising her culinary flair," said Timmy the Winns with an appreciative sniff.

"Aye, I'd know her eggplant stew anywhere," said Griff as they strolled toward the bridge across the river.

Suddenly, Alistair saw a familiar flash of red pacing the bridge, just as Tibby Rose hissed in his ear, "That's the guard who—"

Timmy the Winns turned to see why they had slowed. "Huck? Jim?"

Alistair's throat was dry. "There's . . . there's a guard," he said hesitantly.

But Timmy the Winns just chuckled. "Don't bother him and he won't bother you," he said. And as he led them across the bridge, he began to tell a story about a talking piece of cheese he had met on his travels. "Now the funny thing about this cheese—"

"Was that it could talk!" interrupted Tibby Rose.

"No," said Timmy the Winns. "The funny thing about this talking cheese was that it was riding a bicycle."

"Cheese riding a bicycle?" Tibby Rose dissolved in giggles.

"I tell you it was so," said Timmy the Winns. "Evening, Purkiss," he said, raising a hand to the red-coated guard.

The guard nodded. "Wotcher, Timmy," he replied. "Is that your supper I can smell on the breeze?"

"With any luck, Purkiss, with any luck," said Timmy the Winns as they continued on their way.

And just like that they were on the other side of the river and walking along a tow path toward the blue-striped tent.

They arrived at the camp to see the three younger mice sitting around a merrily crackling fire, bowls of steaming stew in their laps. Watching them fondly was a round mouse with a fringed shawl thrown around her shoulders. Even in the fading light, Alistair could tell that her fur was a deep forest green.

She turned at the sound of their approach. "If you'd been any longer there'd have been naught but dregs for ye," she said laughingly, "the way these wee mites are wolfin' down that stew."

"Ah, Mags," said Griff, "I know you wouldn't let me to starve. And here's some bread to fill those ravenous bellies—plus we've picked up a couple more ravenous bellies in need of stew." He beckoned Alistair and Tibby Rose forward. "Huck, Jim, this is my wife, Mags. You've already met our bairns." He dipped his head at the mice by the fire.

Alistair and Tibby Rose ducked their heads shyly at Mags, who asked them no questions, but handed them each a bowl into which she had ladled a hearty helping of stew. "And very welcome you are," was all she said.

Lilith gestured to them to sit beside her, and the two guests slid onto a log which served as a bench and began to eat while Mags served Griff, Timmy the Winns, and herself.

At first, all Alistair's attention was focused on the stew. He never paid that much attention to food particularly—not the way his brother Alex or Uncle Ebenezer did; they were obsessed—but he had to admit he had never tasted a stew so rich and flavorsome.

"This stew," he gasped, after the first mouthful. "It's delicious! What's in it?"

"Get away, it's nothing special," Mags said, waving away the compliment, but she looked pleased. "It's just my eggplant stew. With some tomatoes and a few wild herbs I gathered here and there."

As Alistair savored the rest of the stew, mopping up the remains as the others did with a piece of bread torn from the loaf, he watched the mice gathered around the fire. Griff, Mags, and the children were a family, but it appeared that Timmy the Winns wasn't part of it. So why was he with them, and why did it seem as if he was somehow their leader?

His musings were interrupted by a hoarse coughing coming from within the tent. The younger mice froze, their eyes fixed on their plates, and as Mags rose from her place by the fire and hurried into the tent, Griff cast Timmy the Winns a guarded look. Alistair opened his mouth to ask who it was that had coughed, but when Timmy the Winns looked over at him, Alistair remembered what he'd said about asking questions and closed his mouth again.

"Poor old Uncle Silas," Timmy murmured, raising his eyebrows at the younger mice, who tittered nervously and nudged each other, saying "Yes, poor Uncle Silas" and "Poor Uncle Silas is so poorly," until Griff silenced them with a stern glance.

When Mags returned to the fireside, she said nothing about Uncle Silas, but asked, "And which of ye terrors wants a piece of my blackberry cobbler?"

Pip, Lilith, and Fergus whooped with pleasure, but Tibby and Alistair looked at each other. "No thanks," they said in unison.

After the cobbler had been demolished they all sat quiet and content around the fire. Before long the three younger mice were asleep and, with a sigh, Griff rose, stretched, and went to fetch a basin of water from the river so he could do the dishes. Mags, after exchanging a glance and nod with Timmy the Winns, slipped into Uncle Silas's tent.

Alistair looked at Tibby. By the light of the flickering flames he could see that her eyes were almost closed and her chin was sinking toward her chest. He was just about to suggest they return to their own "camp" under the willow tree when Timmy the Winns murmured, "Do you know why you're traveling, little brother?"

Alistair, a bit surprised, said, "Yes." He was going home to Smiggins, home to Alice and Alex and his aunt and uncle.

"Have you thought of those you leave behind?" Timmy asked in the same low murmur.

What an odd thing to say. Those he'd left behind were the ones he was traveling toward. Alistair merely nodded.

Timmy looked at Alistair intently, his dark eyes shining in the firelight. "Perhaps you should travel with us," he suggested. "This is no place for two young mice to be wandering."

It seemed to Alistair that the midnight blue mouse looked faintly worried, and he felt a prick of fear—he would have thought nothing could worry Timmy the Winns. Nevertheless, he shook his head. "No," he said. "But thank you." Although it would be safer to travel with Timmy and the others, Alistair knew that he and Tibby would move faster alone.

He glanced at Timmy to see his response, but Timmy was now gazing at Alistair's scarf.

"That's a handsome scarf, my friend," he observed. "It's been a long while since I've seen its like."

Alistair tugged at the ends of the scarf self-consciously. "It was a gift from my mother," he said.

"From your mother," Timmy repeated. Alistair thought he looked almost sad.

Timmy gazed at the scarf for a few moments longer, his eyes roaming over the strange design, then he reached for his fiddle and said, "Just one song ere we part, I think. I'll sing you a song of the Winns . . ."

"What's the Winns?" Alistair asked.

"The Winns," Timmy said dreamily. "The Winns is a river, and more than that. It is the spine that knits our head to our feet. Its veins run through our country and its water runs through our veins." He played a mournful note on the fiddle. "Above the trees, below the ground, the Winns is with you, all around."

He closed his eyes for a moment, and then began to move the bow gently across the strings. After a few notes, he started to sing.

> *"From rock to ridge to tunnel to tree*
> *The songs are there for you to see;*
> *Read the land and follow the signs,*
> *Read the river between the lines."*

Alistair felt his heart stir at the sound of the melancholy melody. It was achingly familiar, yet he could swear he had never heard the song before. He found himself humming as Timmy the Winns sang the refrain.

> *"Wherever the Winns takes me, that's where I'll be,*
> *For me and the Winns will always flow free."*

As the final notes drifted into the night, Alistair sighed with a sadness he couldn't name. It wasn't just homesickness for Smiggins, for his brother and sister and uncle and aunt. It wasn't even for his parents, and their honey-colored house in Stubbins. He felt as if he was homesick for a place he'd never been and maybe would never see.

His reverie was interrupted by Timmy the Winns. "I don't know the whole song," he said. "Not the really important verses." He put the fiddle down. "Ah well, if you are determined to travel your own path it's time you and the lass were away."

Alistair had been worried about how they'd find their way back in the dark, and even more worried about crossing the bridge alone, but Timmy the Winns stood up. "I'll come along for the walk," he said.

Alistair nudged the slumbering Tibby and the two muddy-purple mice rose and thanked Mags, who had just come out of the tent, for the dinner. She smiled and pressed a cloth bag into Alistair's hands. "For your journey," she said. Then, bidding farewell to Mags and Griff—their children were still fast asleep by the glowing embers—Alistair and a sleepy Tibby Rose, accompanied by Timmy the Winns, retraced their steps along the tow path and crossed the bridge with only a drowsy murmur from the guard. Although Alistair had been vague about where they were sleeping, Timmy the Winns stopped as soon as the willow tree by the river's edge was in sight.

"This is where our paths diverge," he said to Alistair. "Safe travels, Huck, and you too, Jim. I warrant our paths will cross again, perhaps when the Winns flows free." And on that cryptic note, he turned and loped away without a backward glance.

Alistair and Tibby Rose stumbled down the bank and parted the fronds of their hidden room. There was their raft, undisturbed. As the long leafy curtains settled into place, the two mice curled up at the base of the tree. Tibby Rose was asleep within minutes, but Alistair lay awake a little longer, thinking of the mysterious Timmy the Winns. Was it just his imagination, or had Timmy the Winns seemed to know him? Or perhaps that was just his nature, Alistair mused. Like his motto about treating every stranger like a friend.

He heard an owl hoot close by, sending a chill through his blood. He hoped the night hunter had not spotted Timmy the Winns.

But a few minutes later he heard the familiar voice drift across the river.

"Wherever the Winns takes me, that's where I'll be,
For me and the Winns will always flow free."

And then he fell asleep.

11

Joining Forces

"What took you so long?" said Sophia.

As the silvery mouse gazed down at Alice and her brother with an amused twinkle in her eye, Alice honestly couldn't tell if the elegant mouse and her morose companion were friends or foes. She held her breath, waiting for what was to come.

But as Sophia rose from the sled and moved to stand over them, Alice saw that her expression was sympathetic.

"You poor dears," she said. "Are you all right?"

"It wasn't so bad," said Alex, brushing ice crystals from his fur.

"Well, I must say," said Sophia, her voice full of admiration, "it was certainly an ingenious way to get down the mountain. How clever you are."

Alex ducked his head modestly. "The idea just kind of came to me . . ."

"The idea came to you?" Alice spluttered. "It was an accid—ooph!" The rest of her sentence was lost as her brother suddenly sat on her.

"Oops, sorry, sis," Alex said. "I didn't mean to sit on you. It was an accident."

"The thing that most troubles me," Sophia continued, "is why you were hiding in that barrel in the first place. Surely it wasn't—" She put a hand to her chest. "You weren't running from *us*, were you?"

The two younger mice nodded sheepishly.

"Oh dear," said Sophia. "Do you hear that, Horace? Alex and Alice thought we were chasing them."

Horace, still sitting on the sled, nodded gloomily.

"Oh no, no, no," said Sophia, shaking her head vigorously. "We have been trying to find you—we've come to help you look for your brother Alistair." She cast a quick glance around the snowy landscape, then said in a low voice, "We're from FIG."

"You are?" Alice felt relief flood through her, warming her frozen body. "Oh that's wonderful. Did Uncle Ebenezer send you to look for Alistair?"

"That's right," said Sophia. "We set off shortly after you did, and we've been trying to catch up with you ever since. I thought taking the shortcut over Mount Sharpnest would put us in front of you, but I didn't imagine us meeting quite like this."

"Oh, it doesn't matter now," said Alice. She felt as if a great weight had been lifted from her shoulders. She hadn't realized before how heavily the responsibility of finding Alistair by themselves had been weighing on her. And if Horace and Sophia had been looking for her and Alex, it meant that their uncle had seen their note—and surely he and Beezer would be less worried, knowing that their niece and nephew were with the two FIG members. "We're just glad you're here. Aren't we, Alex?"

"Yes," said Alex, and Alice could tell he was thinking of goat's cheese omelets. "We sure are."

Smiling warmly, Sophia said, "Before we get back on the road I think you really should have a bite of something to settle your stomachs after that terrifying ordeal."

"That's a great idea!" said Alex, then his face fell as he pulled their rucksack from the bottom of the barrel. "But all we've got is this old dry bread." He fished in the rucksack and produced the remains of the loaf the farmer had given them two days earlier.

"Oh no," said Sophia, regarding it with distaste. "We won't be needing that. Horace?" As Horace stood up and began to wrestle with a large cloth-wrapped parcel sitting in the back of the sled, Sophia explained, "That charming old cheesemaking woodcutter—or was he a woodcutting cheesemaker?—was kind enough to give me a sample from his cellar."

As Horace staggered over clutching the parcel with both arms, Sophia said, "Just flip that barrel over, will you, Alex? We can use it as a table. Thank you, dear."

Alex leaped to the task enthusiastically, and with a grunt Horace hefted the parcel onto the makeshift table.

"Excellent work, Horace—how strong you are." Sophia unwrapped the cloth to reveal half a wheel of cheese with a rough orange rind.

"Ohhh . . . ," breathed Alex reverently.

"Oh, indeed," said Sophia with satisfaction. "Horace, would you fetch a knife from my bag, please?"

Horace handed her the knife, and Sophia proceeded to shave slices of the hard cheese from the wheel, and Alice, Alex, and Sophia ate with relish (Horace proclaimed himself too full of fondue to join in). By the time Sophia said, "I think it's time we resumed the search for your dear brother, don't you?" and Alex had volunteered to carry the woodcutting cheesemaker's excellent cheese in the rucksack, and Sophia had said how thoughtful he was, but why didn't he let Horace carry the rucksack (as well as Sophia's own rather large bag), Alice was feeling quite recovered from their horrible descent down the mountain.

Leaving the sled where it stood—"Macduff knows where to find it," Sophia assured them—they continued on foot. A couple of hours passed, in which they slogged first through snow, then through slush, then through an unpleasant muddy mush. By the time the mountain path had rejoined the main road to the coast, the ground was warm and dry underfoot and they were in a lush green valley with thick forests of chestnut trees covering the hills. The occasional village of golden stone could be glimpsed on the hilltops and a wide green river curved along the valley floor, sometimes running alongside the road before winding away through fields and meadows. They walked for several hours, but the time passed pleasantly for Alice and Alex (though not for Horace, who groaned pitifully beneath the weight of the cheese-laden rucksack). They told Sophia, who was very interested, all about their lives in Smiggins, and in Stubbins before that.

"Four years without your parents," she murmured. "And now your brother missing too." But unlike the farmer, who had thought them very careless to lose so many family members, Sophia was full of sympathy.

It was early evening when Sophia stopped before a sign for the Riverside Inn. "This should do nicely," she declared. "Comfy beds and a good hot dinner for us tonight."

Alex's face brightened at the mention of dinner, but Alice said, "Um, I—I don't think we have enough money for that." She was too embarrassed to tell Sophia that they had set off with no money at all.

"Oh, don't you worry." Sophia waved a hand dismissively. "FIG will pay."

They turned off the road and walked down a short avenue of poplars to a three-story stone building with a long, gently sloping roof. Hedges of rosemary and lavender perfumed the balmy air.

Sophia led them into the reception area and addressed the black and white mouse behind the counter.

"What a charming little hotel you have here," she said sweetly, and the black and white mouse beamed. "These two will have a room on the top floor, please, on the river side of the building, and I'd like a room directly beneath them. Horace here will have a room on the ground floor near the door. (You know you're scared of heights, dear.) And where is your restaurant?"

The black and white mouse, who was busily pulling keys from a board on the wall behind him, said, "Straight through there, madam." He indicated a door leading to the back of the hotel. "On a lovely evening like this, I'd recommend you take your dinner on the terrace. We have a lovely view of the river."

"That sounds perfectly delightful," said Sophia in her bell-like voice. "If you give the keys to Horace he can take our bags up to our rooms. We three will go straight out to the terrace to consider the menu."

The view from the terrace was as good as the innkeeper had promised, and Alice thought she had never seen a lovelier spot as she sat beneath the plane trees shading their table and gazed at the forested hills on the far bank.

Sophia and Alex, meanwhile, were engaged in a lively discussion of the menu.

By the time Horace joined them, they had decided on the local specialty, which was a disgusting-sounding dish of thin, wriggly baby eels with a blue cheese sauce. The black and white mouse came to take their order— his wife, he assured them, was renowned as one of the region's finest chefs—and Alice and Horace, less adventurous than the other two, ordered macaroni and cheese.

As they ate their meal, Alice, who was feeling too tired to join in the conversation led by Sophia, sat quietly and observed their new traveling companions. Horace seemed determinedly glum, and didn't engage much with Alice and Alex, but Sophia was quite a different character. Even though the younger mice had already told her all about themselves, she carried on asking question after question ("And where did your parents say they were going?" "Do your aunt and uncle travel much?" "Do they have many friends?") and Alice noticed that although she was light and pleasant at all times, and seemed very casual about her questioning, she listened intently to their answers with a shrewd gleam in her eye—as if she wasn't being quite so casual after all. . . .

"Alex," said Alice, when they had returned to their room after dinner, leaving Horace and Sophia to finish their coffee on the terrace, "there's something not quite right about Sophia. Why did she ask us so many questions?"

Alex, stretched out on his bed beneath the window, snorted. "Give it a rest, sis. Horace is a bit strange, I'll grant you, but there's nothing wrong with Sophia. She finds us very interesting—and who can blame her? Anyway, isn't eating in restaurants and sleeping in hotels better than eating dry bread in a cave?"

Alice glared at him. "Would you stop thinking with your stomach for one minute and listen to me? What about the fact that Sophia said they'd set off shortly after we did, but Mr. Grudge told us he'd seen a gray mouse and a black one in his garden with a ladder? If they only found out about us from Uncle Ebenezer after we'd left, what were they doing in the garden earlier that morning?"

"If you're trying to prove they're the kidnappers," Alex argued, "answer this: Why are they helping us to look for Alistair? They should already have him. And who knows? Maybe Mr. Grudge saw different gray and black mice in his lettuce patch."

"Oh, I see," said Alice through gritted teeth. "You're suggesting there are two pairs of gray and black mice roaming around Shetlock looking for Alistair?"

Alex shrugged. "It's possible, isn't it?"

Alice thumped her pillow in frustration. She was sure there was something suspicious about Sophia. Why couldn't her brother see it? Well, he could do what he liked, but she would be keeping an eye on the silvery Sophia. . . .

"Could you close the shutters, Alex?" she complained. "I can't sleep with the light in my eyes."

"All right, all right, keep your fur on." Kneeling up on his bed, Alex leaned out the window toward the shutters. He began to laugh. "Hey, sis, check this out— Horace has a bald patch."

Alice forgot she was cross with him and hopped out of bed to join him at the window.

"Ha! He does too. I never noticed that before. Maybe

he brushes his fur over to cover it?"

Almost as if he knew they were talking about him, Horace ran a hand over the fur on his head, then they heard him say: "First we're sent to Smiggins, then we're told, 'Oh no, you have to go to Stubbins now.'" His voice sounded whiny. "We were told that all we had to do was follow his brother and sister and we'd find the ginger one. Now we've been walking for days and it turns out they have no idea where he is."

"Horace, Horace," said Sophia patiently. "You really must learn to relax—go with the flow. Alex and Alice seem set on going to Shambles, so we'll go to Shambles with them. If there's no sign of their brother there . . . *pffft*." She flicked a finger as if dispatching an annoying insect. "We'll get rid of them. Permanently."

12

The Waterfall

Alistair woke from a dream in which two columns of red-coated mice were advancing on him as he lay in a blue-striped tent with his arms pinned to the ground by giant boulders. With an enormous sigh of relief he recognized the green fronds of the willow tree.

He turned his head to see Tibby Rose lying on her back a few meters away, fast asleep.

It was when he lifted his arm to lever himself up that Alistair realized why he had been dreaming about having enormous weights on his arms; they were so stiff he could barely move them.

He lay still, contemplating a life without the use of his

arms, until he heard a snuffling snore and then: "I'd get up," Tibby Rose said, "but I can't actually lift my arms."

"I know," said Alistair ruefully. "That'll teach us to behave like Olympic paddlers."

"Please tell me we don't have to go on the raft again today."

"I wish I could," said Alistair, "but . . . "

"Couldn't we walk?"

"Too slow."

Tibby sighed. "At least tell me we don't have to eat blackberries for breakfast. Given the way we look I'd feel like a cannibal."

"Ah, I've got some good news on that front." With a groan Alistair put a hand to the ground and pushed himself upright, then reached for the cloth bag Mags had handed him the night before. "We've got bread, cheese, strawberries and—what's this? Mmm . . . two pieces of apple pie."

"That sounds lovely . . . But could you feed me, please? I don't think I'll be able to lift my hand to my mouth."

Alistair extended a hand and, moaning, Tibby let him pull her up. "You'll feel better once you're moving," he promised. "Our muscles just need warming up. Now what do you want for breakfast?"

"Apple pie," said Tibby Rose promptly. When Alistair

raised his eyebrows she shrugged. "I can't say that Great-Aunt Harriet would approve, but so what? Great-Aunt Harriet isn't here. She's stuck at home covered in purple spots." Tibby chewed the piece of apple pie Alistair had handed her. "I wonder how she'll explain her miracle cure after so many years."

As his friend ate, Alistair recalled the words of Timmy the Winns the night before: *Do you know why you're traveling . . . Have you thought of those you leave behind?* Alistair had immediately thought of his own family, but what about Tibby's? With a sudden pang he remembered kindly Grandpa Nelson and fierce Great-Aunt Harriet, so determined to protect Tibby Rose that they wouldn't let her leave the house, and were seemingly prepared to give up their own freedom. And now she was gone. How must they be feeling?

"Tibby," he said, "Timmy the Winns asked me the strangest questions last night. He asked me if I knew why I was traveling, and if I had thought about those I left behind. At first I thought of Shetlock and my family—that I was traveling to them because I had left them behind. But . . . I think he might have been asking more than that. I mean, if I think about why I'm so anxious to get home, it's really to do with my parents. When they went away and never came back. . . ." He paused, trying to think of the words that would describe the pain he had

162

felt, but no words seemed adequate. "It was awful," he said finally. "I decided that I never wanted to cause pain like that to people I love. I suppose it's made me a bit too cautious."

Tibby shook her head. "With me it's the opposite," she said. "I know that Grandpa Nelson and Great-Aunt Harriet were trying to protect me, but you can't hold people back because you're scared of them getting hurt, or you're scared of getting hurt yourself. Taking risks is part of life, and so is getting hurt. People have to live their own lives." She was silent for a moment, and Alistair wondered if, despite her brave words, she was thinking of the two old mice she'd left behind. Then she said briskly, "We might as well get moving." She stood and brushed the crumbs from her fur.

When they left the shelter of the willow tree, Alistair saw that the weather had changed. The sky was low with brooding clouds the same bruised, muddy color as their fur.

"Alistair," Tibby said, as they launched the raft and maneuvered into the current, "why didn't you tell Timmy the Winns our real names? Didn't you trust him? I thought he and Griff and Mags and the rest were all really nice."

"It wasn't that I didn't trust him," Alistair said, settling into a slow, regular stroke as Tibby kept them on course with the steering pole. "I did trust him, I think . . . I just had a sense that he didn't want to know our secrets. Or that maybe he already knew them. I mean, he knew straight away that our names were fake."

"Telling him my name was Jim probably didn't help," said Tibby Rose.

"I was put on the spot," Alistair protested. "I couldn't think of anything else. But anyway, he just laughed, and he didn't ask for our real names. And then I wondered . . . Tibby, did you notice his arms? They were his real fur, not dyed like the rest of him, and it was hard to tell because there was such a swirl of colors, but I think I saw some ginger."

"Ginger?" Tibby's eyes were wide. "But he can't be like us. I mean, remember how friendly the guard was?"

"Yeah, but he is dyed, isn't he? Like us . . . " Alistair started thinking again about Timmy the Winns's ironic smile; how he looked at Alistair as if the two of them shared a secret. Tibby, too, seemed lost in her own thoughts, and so they drifted down the river without speaking.

When his stomach told him it was lunchtime, Alistair tore some bread from the loaf and handed it to Tibby, who murmured her thanks, and early in the afternoon they pulled into a small pebbly beach to rest their arms and stretch their legs, before setting off again. As they pushed off from the beach, they felt the first spatters of rain, and within a few minutes it was pouring, rain streaming down their whiskers and soaking their fur. Alistair scanned the river's banks for shelter, dashing raindrops from his eyes, but there was no shelter to be had. They had no choice but to continue on in the hope of finding a place to stop further downriver.

Shivering as a slight wind chilled his damp fur, Alistair tried to think of something other than his discomfort. His mind worried at the big, unsolved mystery which had led to him rafting down this river: How did he get to Templeton in the first place? He was pretty sure by now that he wasn't trapped in an exceptionally long-running and vivid dream. He supposed it was possible that he was mad and his whole adventure in Souris was one grand delusion (that would certainly explain the fact that he had seen yellow and green and orange and scarlet and blue mice), but he didn't *feel* mad. (Then again, if you were mad you probably didn't know it.) What about magic? Alistair wasn't inclined to believe in magic, but at the moment he was feeling hard pressed to come up with another explanation. Still, if he had been transported to Souris by an act of magic, what was its purpose? He didn't think it likely that magicians or wizards or witches just wandered around practicing random acts of magic, and his sudden appearance in Souris was nothing if not random.

Alistair sighed and shook the water from his face. Maybe he'd never know. . . .

"We must be getting near the lake," Tibby remarked. The banks were so high they could see nothing of the countryside they were passing through, but the current was growing noticeably swifter. She gestured with her pole to a rocky outcrop on the left bank. "Perhaps we should stop over by those rocks. Maybe if we climb the bank, we'll be able to see how far away the lake is."

"Sounds like a plan," said Alistair, and he rowed hard to the right with his paddle to steer them toward the left bank.

"Hey, Tib," he said after a few minutes in which he didn't seem to be making any impact on the direction of the raft, "can you give us a push with the pole? I'm having a bit of trouble getting us to the side."

"I *am* pushing," Tibby said. "As hard as I can. The current's too strong. Anyway, we'll be close to the side soon enough—look at how the river's narrowing up ahead."

The river was getting ever faster, the raft rocking on the current. Alistair felt a sudden thrill of fear between his shoulder blades as he heard what sounded like a distant roar.

"Tibby," he called, as the roar became louder, "what's that sound?"

He didn't hear her reply. "What?" he shouted. "I can't hear you!"

"Waterfall!" came his friend's urgent reply. "We're headed for a waterfall!"

They were bucking and bouncing now as the water churned around them. Tibby was thrown off-balance and fell to her knees where she remained, still clutching the now useless pole. As water washed over the raft, Alistair, paddling frantically to no avail, watched with regret as the cloth bag containing the remainder of Mags's provisions was swept overboard. Then it occurred to him that they themselves might be swept overboard— and if not, that they were about to be plunged over what might be a very high drop. He was wondering if it would be better to jump overboard rather than hurtle to their deaths on their flimsy craft when, with a sense of dread, he remembered that Tibby couldn't swim. He knew that he couldn't abandon her after everything they'd been through, which meant they had only one option: they would go over the waterfall together.

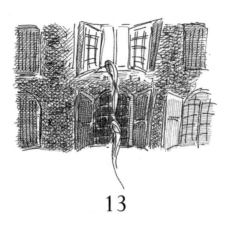

13

Sourian Spies

Alice grabbed her brother's arm. "*Get rid of them? Did she mean—?*"

"Shhh." Alex flapped a hand to shush her. "I'm trying to listen."

Below them, Horace shivered. "They're only children, Sophia."

"They're *Gerandan* children, Horace, the children of spies, and they'll grow up to be members of that frightful FIG. Don't forget who you work for, dear. We'll be in enough trouble as it is for allowing the ginger brat to slip through our fingers. I just wish I knew who had him. From what those two say the aunt and uncle haven't a clue, which suggests that FIG has nothing to do with his disappearance." She pointed her breadstick at her companion. "It's a mystery, Horace, and I don't like mysteries—unless I've caused them myself."

She rose from her chair, stretched her slender arms above her head, and gave a little yawn. "I suppose we'd better turn in. We've got a long walk ahead of us tomorrow. I'll check that the little dears are safely tucked up in their beds before I go to my room. And you will keep a watch on the front door, won't you, Horace? Just in case they should take it into their heads to slip off without us."

"Of course, Sophia," said Horace dismally. "Don't worry about me. I don't need sleep."

"There's a dear," said Sophia, and with a wave of her dainty hand she disappeared inside.

"Quick," Alice hissed. "Close the shutters and then get under the covers and pretend you're asleep."

She scampered back to her bed and climbed beneath the sheet, then waited with her heart pounding for Sophia to appear.

Minutes later they heard Sophia's light footsteps coming up the corridor. Then the door opened and a crack of light shone in, hitting Alice's face. Although her pulse was racing, Alice did her best to keep her breaths deep and regular and her eyelids motionless. From his bed under the window Alex gave a snore. Then the door closed and they heard a fumbling at the lock before Sophia's footsteps could be heard retreating down the hall to the staircase.

"Alex," Alice said in a small voice, "who has the key to the room?"

"I don't know," said Alex's voice in the dark. "I think Horace had it. He took it when he brought our rucksack up."

"I don't think he has it anymore," said Alice. Slipping out of bed she hurried over to the door and tried the handle. "We're locked in!"

"Whoa," said Alex. "This is not good."

"We have to get out of here," Alice said in a rush. "I'm scared."

"But even if we could get out, Horace is watching the front door," Alex replied.

"What about the window then?"

Alex shook his head. "It's too high," he said. "Unless we had some kind of rope . . . " He looked around the room as if there might be a convenient coil of rope lying around. "I know." He slipped off the bed and tugged at his sheet until it came free of the mattress.

"Not long enough," he said. "Give me your sheet, sis."

"Do you think the old tying-sheets-to-make-a-rope trick really works?" said Alice, as she watched her brother knotting the two sheets together.

"Have you got a better idea?" Alex demanded.

"No."

"Then keep quiet and let me do this."

Alice kept quiet until she remembered another problem: "Sophia has the room under ours." She shook her head in despair. "She really has thought of everything. If we go out the window, we'll have to climb down right past her window."

Alex paused and rubbed his chin. Finally he shrugged. "Well, I can't think of another way out. We'll just have to wait till she's asleep and climb down as quietly as we can—and then run for it."

He resumed work, tying one end of the makeshift rope to the bedhead, tugging to make sure the knot would hold.

"That should do it," he said. "How long do you reckon we should wait?"

Alice shook her head. "I don't know . . . an hour?"

They lay on their beds in silence, struggling to stay awake as they waited for the hour to pass. Sophia's words replayed over and over in Alice's mind. *We'll get rid of them . . . ginger brat . . . They're Gerandan children, the children of spies. . . .* She felt a cold chill run down her spine and sat up abruptly.

"Let's go."

Very quietly, Alex eased open the shutters and leaned over the window ledge. "Okay," he said in a whisper, "her light's off." He slowly fed the tied sheets out the window, then turned to face his sister. "There might be a bit of a drop at the bottom if the rope doesn't reach all the way down, but it shouldn't be too bad. I'll go first. When I give you the thumbs-up, throw me the rucksack, then you climb down."

He gave a last tug of the sheet where it was tied to the bedhead, then slipped off the window ledge.

Alice watched anxiously as he descended. The white sheets seemed to glow against the wall, drawing attention to their escape attempt.

She peered into the dark as Alex slipped silently past Sophia's window, half expecting to hear a shout as they were discovered.

At last he was standing on the terrace, and Alice could just make out his thumbs-up. She lifted the rucksack and dropped it into his outstretched arms. There was a faint *oomph* as he caught it. Then it was her turn to descend.

She climbed onto the windowsill. It looked like a long way down. Her hand was trembling as she clutched the rope. She closed her other hand around the rope and, holding it tight, dropped off the ledge. She swung in the air for a moment, the flagstones of the terrace spinning dizzily, then her feet touched the wall of the hotel and she was able to steady herself. One hand after the other, knees gripping the rope, she inched down. She resisted the impulse to shut her eyes as she passed Sophia's window, concentrating instead on her careful progress. It seemed like ages before she felt Alex grab her knees. She let go of the rope, and he lowered her to the ground.

Alex slung the rucksack over one shoulder, and they crept around the side of the hotel to the road.

"Okay," he said, "let's get out of here."

They began to run, anxious to put as much distance as possible between themselves and the treacherous Sophia and Horace.

Once they were out of sight of the hotel, and the rush of adrenaline from their narrow escape began to ease, they slowed their pace to a steady jog, glancing behind them frequently to make sure they weren't being followed.

When she felt like her legs could no longer carry her, Alice gasped, "I need to stop for a minute, Alex." Her lungs were burning as she stood by the side of the road, hands on her knees, panting for breath.

Alex, who didn't appear out of breath in the slightest, looked at her with concern. "Are you all right, sis?"

Alice straightened. "Yes . . . no . . . I don't know. I feel like we're further from finding Alistair than ever. If Sophia and Horace are Sourian agents and they don't have him, then who does? And who do you suppose told them to follow us?"

Alex dropped the rucksack to the ground and rolled his shoulders to ease the muscles. "I don't know. Queen Eugenia?"

"Queen Eugenia?" It didn't seem possible to Alice that the Queen of Souris could possibly be interested in the doings of two young mice from Smiggins in Shetlock. But something wasn't right. The two spies seemed to know too much about them. "Maybe we're going the wrong way," said Alice. "We should go back to Smiggins. What if Uncle Ebenezer and Aunt Beezer are in danger? What if Horace and Sophia didn't know for sure that Uncle Ebenezer and Aunt Beezer had been in contact with FIG, and they were trying to trap us into admitting it? Oh no!" Alice put her hands to her cheeks. "I can't believe we've been so stupid! If we had said 'What's FIG?' they wouldn't have known for sure that Beezer and Ebenezer had anything to do with it. But we as good as admitted that the whole family was part of it. What if, while we're in Shambles, Horace and Sophia decide to go back to interrogate our aunt and uncle about the resistance?"

Alex, who looked like he was having trouble following Alice's disordered thoughts, argued, "But what about Alistair? What if he *is* in Shambles and Sophia and Horace go there and find him?"

Alice covered her eyes with her hands and shook her head. "I don't know what to do," she wailed. "Who's in more danger: Alistair, or Beezer and Ebenezer?"

"Or us?" added Alex, glancing back down the road. "Look, their first priority seems to be Alistair, so I think he should be our first priority too. Besides, Beezer and Ebenezer have each other, and Alistair only has us to help him."

And so it was decided. They'd continue on to Shambles.

14

The Mouse from Gerander

Alistair swiped an impatient hand over his eyes. It was almost impossible to see through the rain and the mist rising from the waterfall, but the deafening roar in his ears told him the waterfall was very close. The raft was rocking violently from side to side as the river surged toward the precipice ahead. He was about to shout to Tibby to hold on, that they were going over, when he noticed her edging determinedly toward the front of the raft on her knees, holding the pole horizontally in both hands at chest height.

"Grab onto the pole!" she yelled above the thunder of the water. Without hesitation Alistair dropped his paddle and did as he was told. As the raft shot through a narrow rocky chute on a crest of tumbling water, the pole held firm across the chasm, the two mice flung against it by the force of the torrent.

For several minutes, they did nothing but cling to the pole, buffeted by the relentless rush of water. Then, at a nudge from Tibby, Alistair began to edge to the right, where the pole rested on a narrow platform of rock at the base of a steep cliff.

Minutes later the two sodden mice collapsed, panting, onto the rock. Alistair lay face down, his heart pounding, still feeling the terror of their close shave.

"We lost the raft," Tibby said sorrowfully, when she had caught her breath enough to speak.

"Things could be worse," Alistair joked weakly. "At least we're not ginger."

Sure enough, despite their thorough soaking, they were still a muddy purple.

Eventually, Alistair sat up. He took his scarf from around his neck and wrung it out, then got to his feet. His limbs were shaky with adrenaline.

"How are you feeling, Tib?" he asked.

Tibby Rose turned her head to look at him. Her eyes were wide. "Scared stiff," she said. "If that makes any sense *after* the fact."

"I know exactly what you mean," Alistair assured her.

"But do you feel up to a gentle afternoon stroll—to the top of this rock face?"

"Oh, an afternoon stroll," said Tibby, flexing her limbs experimentally. "Delighted, I'm sure."

"After you," said Alistair politely, gesturing at the cliff.

"So kind," said Tibby.

The storm clouds were drifting away to the east, and the rain had eased to a light sprinkle, but their journey up the wet rock face was a perilous one. Fortunately, there were plenty of handholds and footholds, though once Alistair's foot slipped and set his heart pounding all over again. He tried to keep his mind empty, focusing on the next placement of his foot, the next spur for his hand to grip. Right hand. Left foot. Left hand. Right foot. At last he was flinging himself over the top onto a grassy bank.

"Lovely stroll, thanks," said Tibby, standing over him with her hands on her hips. "I hope you're planning to offer me afternoon tea next."

Alistair rolled onto his back and slapped his forehead with his palm. "I knew I forgot something," he said. "I left the picnic basket at the bottom of the cliff. You could go back for it . . . ?"

Tibby laughed. "No way," she said. "Let's just admire the view instead."

Alistair got to his feet. Stretching away before him was a huge egg-shaped lake—Lake Eugenia, he presumed. The water was a steely gray, reflecting the sky, and around its shore were dotted little settlements, clusters of red-tiled roofs. On the far side of the lake was a mountain range, a jagged row of sharp teeth silhouetted against the sky. To his left was the waterfall they had so nearly plunged over. Alistair gasped when he saw how high it was. There was no way they would have survived.

"That's where we need to go."

Alistair glanced down to where Tibby was pointing. Directly beneath them was a road, and to Alistair's relief the incline was of loose gravel rather than treacherous rock. They half ran, half slid down the hill, arriving breathless at the bottom. Stretching away on the other side of the road were vineyards, the vines heavy with purple grapes. Food! Alistair plucked a plum-colored globe from a vine and popped it into his mouth, but instead of the tart juicy tang he was expecting, the grape was sour and bitter.

"Yuck," he said, spitting it out.

Tibby giggled. "Those aren't the eating kind," she told him. "They're for making wine."

"They're horrible," said Alistair. "I don't know why anyone would drink wine if it tastes like that."

"I think we should make it our policy never to eat anything purple again," said Tibby, looking at her fur. "I am *so* over purple."

As they trudged along the road past vine after vine of inedible grapes, Alistair said, "What made you think of putting the pole between the two banks like that?"

"It was in Charlotte Tibby's survival handbook," said Tibby. "In the chapter on surviving waterfalls."

"When we get home I'm going to write Charlotte Tibby a fan letter," said Alistair. "If you hadn't read her book we'd probably still be sitting by the river in Templeton."

"Go right ahead," said Tibby Rose. "Address it to the cemetery in Grouch. Charlotte Tibby died about fifty years ago."

"Her advice has certainly stood the test of time then. What does she say you should do when you're caught out in the rain?" Alistair asked as the clouds above opened in another downpour.

"Seek shelter," Tibby called, and she took off down the road at a run.

They had been running through the rain for about a quarter of an hour, and were so drenched Alistair wasn't quite sure why they were bothering to run, when he spotted a small square building a short way off the road, surrounded by rows of vines.

"Over there, Tib." He led the way through the vines to what looked like a blank white box with a rough-cut opening for a door and two tiny windows. A few dry brown trails of ivy leaves straggled up one side, and the tiled roof had plenty of gaps. Alistair guessed that this must be some kind of shed, probably only used during harvest time given its general air of abandonment and neglect. The trough of water alongside must have been fed by an underground spring, though, for when Alistair dipped his hand in and raised it to his lips, the water tasted fresh and sweet.

He looked in the door. It was almost dark in the shed, with not much light filtering through the grimy window, and the air smelled damp and musty. Alistair, his eyes not yet accustomed to the dim light, struggled to make out some plastic containers stacked on the dirt floor, a couple of buckets (one with a broken handle) and, leaning against the wall beside the door, a rusty pruning saw. In the far corner was a heap of old sacks.

"Coast is clear, Tib," he called over his shoulder, and she joined him in the doorway, where they shook the water from their fur as best they could and Alistair wrung out his scarf again.

"I hope we don't have to stay here too long," Tibby said, wrinkling her nose. "It smells kind of moldy."

Suddenly there was a hoarse cough, quickly muffled.

The two mice froze.

"Who—who's there?" Alistair demanded in a quavering voice.

There was no answer, but as Alistair's eyes adjusted to the gloom he saw a trembling shape in the corner, huddled under a thin blanket. Then the trembling shape coughed again and Alistair remembered where he'd heard that cough before.

"Uncle Silas!" he cried. "You were in the tent last night, with Timmy the Winns and Griff and Mags."

"I don't know what you're talking about," said the huddled shape, but he sat up.

Alistair saw an old, thin mouse with round spectacles. "So you're not Uncle Silas, then?" Alistair asked.

"I most certainly am not," said the old mouse.

"And you weren't in Pamplemouse yesterday?"

"I've never heard of it."

"Oh. Well, what are you doing in this shed?"

"What are *you* doing here?" the other mouse countered.

Alistair and Tibby exchanged looks. "We're, ah, traveling," said Alistair.

"So am I," said the old mouse. "But you two look a bit young to be traveling about on your own. You—" Before he could finish his sentence his frail body was racked with a terrible coughing fit.

"Oh," Tibby cried. "Alistair, help him—fetch some water."

Alistair peered out the door to check that there was no one about, then darted around the corner to the trough. He was just casting about for something to carry the water in when he spied a tin mug hanging from a hook on the trough's outer edge. He filled the cup and then carried it carefully back to the shed.

The old mouse was hunched over, the blanket around his shoulders, and Tibby Rose was kneeling beside him patting him gently on the back.

Alistair crouched before him and held out the mug.

The old mouse took it in his shaking hands and drank. "Thank you," he said at last, and his voice sounded stronger now.

"Are you ill?" Tibby asked, sounding worried.

The mouse shrugged. "I'm old, and I have traveled a long, long way," he said. "My health is a small concern compared to the importance of my mission."

"You're on a mission?" said Alistair. "What mission? For who?"

The old mouse snorted. "And why would I trust you with that information?"

Alistair paused. The old mouse was right; he had no reason to trust them, just as they had no reason to trust him. And yet Alistair felt sure that this was the mouse who Timmy the Winns had called Uncle Silas (though Alistair doubted that was his real name), and that any friend of Timmy the Winns would do them no harm. Indeed, they might be able to help each other. Like

Alistair and Tibby Rose, this old mouse had reason to hide. Like them, he had reason to be watchful and cautious. Was it possible that their reasons were related? Did he have the answers to some of their questions? Alistair looked into the old mouse's eyes. If he wanted Uncle Silas to trust him, he would have to make the first move.

"Well, I trust you," Alistair told Uncle Silas. "Enough to tell you our secret."

He glanced at Tibby, who gave him a small nod.

"We're on the run," Alistair began. "You see we're . . . we're ginger."

"You're ginger?!" The old mouse sat up straight and the blanket fell from his shoulders.

Alistair took a step backward, suddenly regretting his admission.

But the old mouse was beaming. "Where are you from, my friends?"

"I'm from Smiggins, in Shetlock," said Alistair.

"And I'm from Templeton, to the north of here," added Tibby Rose.

The old mouse peered suspiciously from Alistair to Tibby and back again. "The light isn't very good in here, but even so you don't look ginger. Are you trying to fool an old mouse, is that your game?"

"No!" Tibby protested. "We wouldn't do that. We dyed ourselves with blackberries so the Queen's Guards would stop chasing us. And other mice called us terrible names. Although we don't really know what's wrong with being ginger," she confessed.

The old mouse's expression softened, and he pulled the blanket around his shoulders once more.

"If you ask me," he said, "there's nothing wrong at all with a ginger mouse. Indeed, some of the bravest, most heroic mice I have ever known were ginger. And some of the dearest to my heart . . . " He seemed lost in thought for a few minutes, then asked abruptly: "Do either of you know where Gerander is?"

"Of course," said Tibby Rose. "It's a province to the south of—"

"NO!" interrupted the old mouse loudly. Then he shut his eyes and drew a deep breath. When he opened his eyes he said quietly, "No. Gerander isn't a province of Souris—it's a country in its own right. At least, it was . . . "

He took off his spectacles and polished them on a corner of the blanket, as if gathering his thoughts, then resumed.

"How much do you know about Gerander?"

Tibby shook her head. "Great-Aunt Harriet taught me a lot of history, but she never really mentioned Gerander."

"We hardly learned anything about Gerander at school," Alistair said with a shrug. "It was just mentioned as part of Souris."

"Hmph," said the old mouse under his breath. "It's true what they say: history is written by the victors."

"Pardon?" said Alistair, who didn't understand.

The old mouse smiled grimly. "There is really no such thing as 'the truth' when it comes to history. There are always other versions. So while Sourians—and, perhaps, Shetlockers—truly believe that Gerander is part of Souris, the Gerandans themselves see the situation in a very different light."

"Are *you* from Gerander?" Alistair wanted to know.

"I am," said the old mouse defiantly.

"The other day, some mice who were chasing us called me and Tibby 'Gerandan rebels,'" Alistair told him. "What did they mean?"

"Was this before you dyed yourselves?"

"Yes."

The old mouse nodded slowly. "I see. Well, it's time someone told you the truth about Gerander: the truth as Gerandans see it, I should say. The story really starts generations ago. Queen Cornolia—I suppose you've heard of her?"

"Yes," said the two younger mice in unison.

"Queen Cornolia was Queen Eugenia's great-great-grandmother," said Tibby Rose. "She was the Queen of Souris a long time ago."

"And she was the Queen of Shetlock, too," added Alistair.

The old mouse nodded. "That's right. But there was no such thing as Souris or Shetlock in Queen Cornolia's day. They were part of one big kingdom called Greater Gerander, and had been ruled by the House of Cornolius for more generations than history records. But that changed when Queen Cornolia was on her deathbed. She had triplets, you see, and since none was the clear heir, she divided the kingdom into three lands—the countries we now call Souris, Shetlock, and Gerander—each with its own sovereign. For years the three lands coexisted in relative harmony—relative, I say, for what siblings don't squabble from time to time?"

Alistair thought of Alice and Alex, and nodded.

"Anyway, years and years ago—when I was very young—there was an earthquake in Gerander. A *terrible* earthquake! Whole towns were swallowed by the earth, thousands were killed and many more thousands were injured. What hospitals were left couldn't cope with the number of wounded, and there was not enough shelter for those who had lost their homes."

He cleared his throat, and even in the dim light Alistair could see that his eyes were clouded behind his spectacles.

"Now, Gerander was at that time ruled by King Martain, and he sought help from our nearest and much larger neighbor, Souris, ruled by King Erandus—Queen

Eugenia's father. Erandus sent his army to help. They repaired roads and built new houses; they fixed the drainage and the hospitals and the schools. Truly, they were our saviors. But when Gerander was fully restored, King Erandus's army refused to leave! Erandus insisted that Martain had ceded sovereignty of the kingdom of Gerander to the ruler of Souris until such a time as order had been restored and, in his opinion, order had not yet been restored. Martain disputed this version of events, but it was his word against Erandus's—and Erandus, with his huge army, had the advantage. The friends who had once been our saviors were now our occupiers, and so it has remained to this day, though Erandus and Martain are long since dead. But despite the fact we are ruled by Queen Eugenia, Gerander is no province of Souris. Gerander was an independent country—and will be again." These last words were spoken so vehemently that the old mouse was momentarily short of breath.

"I don't understand," said Alistair. "Why would King Erandus want to take over Gerander?"

The old mouse shrugged his thin shoulders. "What does any large country want with a small country? Its land, its wealth . . . Why I bet you didn't know that the produce of all the farms of Gerander is sent to Souris, with only a tiny fraction remaining in our country to feed our people. We are close to starvation, so meager are our rations! But we are told that we must give up our crops in return for the 'services' of the Sourian army."

"But that's awful!" cried Tibby Rose. "Surely if Queen Eugenia knew how the Gerandans suffered . . ."

The old mouse laughed bitterly. "If Queen Eugenia knew? Of course she knows. General Ashwover of the Sourian army is the most powerful man in Gerander, and he reports directly to Queen Eugenia herself."

Alistair shook his head. "It seems like an awful lot of trouble to go to for the produce of some farmland."

"True," the old mouse sighed, "it's more complicated than that. While Gerander is only a thin ribbon of land, it is of great strategic importance. For one thing, although Souris has ports on the Sourian Sea, Gerander's coastline on the Cannolian Ocean gives Souris access to an ocean port, expanding greatly their potential for trade with countries that lie across the Cannolian to the west. It also gives them a land border with Shetlock."

He fell silent, his chin sunk onto his chest, and just as Alistair was wondering if the old mouse had fallen asleep, he shook himself and spoke again. "There's something else, of course. There are some powerful mice in Souris who believe that the kingdom of Greater Gerander should be reunited once more, that the capital of Gerander should once more be home to the House of

Cornolius. And who is left from the House of Cornolius to rule Greater Gerander?"

"Queen Eugenia," Tibby Rose breathed.

"Correct," said the old mouse, and it occurred to Alistair that he might have been a teacher at one time. "But she is not the only one. . . . "

"Who else could there be?" said Alistair, puzzled. "Shetlock doesn't have kings and queens anymore; the last queen gave up her throne so that Shetlockers could decide who would govern them. Since then we vote for a president instead. And you said that Gerander is ruled by Queen Eugenia now."

"You might recall me saying that some of the most heroic mice I have ever known were ginger?"

Alistair and Tibby Rose nodded. Alistair had been hoping the old Gerandan would return to the subject of ginger mice.

"Well, one of these ginger heroes is a mouse by the name of . . . ," and the old mouse's voice seemed to fill with pride and awe as he uttered the name, "Zanzibar."

"Who's Zanzibar?" Alistair wanted to know.

"Zanzibar is the son of the daughter of King Martain. And he is the rightful heir to the kingdom of Gerander. Of course, this has made him the sworn enemy of Queen Eugenia and General Ashwover. Zanzibar has lived most of his life in hiding—and in prison. But he has never given up the fight to free our homeland. Indeed, it is he who started FIG."

"FIG?"

"It stands for Free and Independent Gerander; we are a resistance movement."

He had said "we," Alistair noted. Alistair was surprised and moved to think of a mouse so old and frail fighting bravely for the freedom of his people.

"But in recent years we have suffered some serious setbacks," the old mouse said heavily. "Sourian spies infiltrated the movement and many of us were captured and imprisoned—myself and Zanzibar included. That was ten years ago. Six years we passed in the dungeon of Atticus Island, before being moved to a prison camp in the Cranken Alps on the border of Gerander and Souris." The old mouse closed his eyes and shuddered, as if the memory of the last ten years was too awful to contemplate.

"Five nights ago," he whispered, "a dozen of us escaped from the Cranken prison. A dozen of us attempted to escape, I should say. Only half a dozen made it." The old mouse's voice was very low now. "I was one of the lucky ones. Zanzibar too. But my wife . . ." The old mouse trailed off.

"Maybe get him some more water, Alistair," Tibby Rose suggested softly.

Alistair took the mug, which sat by the old Gerandan's knee, and darted outside to refill it at the trough.

When he returned the old mouse was saying, "Our children, now grown, are scattered I know not where. They were brought up by their grandparents while my wife and I were away working for FIG. I can only hope they understand. . . . Sometimes the needs of the many outweigh the needs of the few."

"I'm sure they would understand," Tibby Rose reassured him.

As Alistair placed the cup in the old mouse's hand, he said, "But I still don't understand what being ginger's got to do with anything."

The old mouse took a long draught of water and then replied, "Don't you see? Only Gerandans are ginger. Not every Gerandan, mind you, but it's not uncommon. The triplet who inherited Gerander from Queen Cornolia was ginger, and there have been ginger Gerandans in every generation since."

"But we're not Gerandan," Alistair pointed out.

"So you say." The old mouse shook his head. "But if you are ginger, then you are Gerandan. That's all there is to it. Maybe your parents are Gerandan, or their parents were."

Alistair thought of Uncle Ebenezer's stories about his and Rebus's boyhood adventures. They had all taken place in Shetlock. What about his mother's childhood? He couldn't remember his mother ever talking about it. Now he regretted that he had never asked.

"It explains why those kids by the river in Templeton were calling us Gerandan rebels, anyway," Tibby said. "And why the mice in town thought we might be spies."

The old mouse ran his hands over his face wearily. "They are good at hating, the Sourians," he said.

"Why have you come to Souris?" Alistair asked. "It must be incredibly dangerous."

"I have important news for FIG members here," the Gerandan replied shortly. "That's all I'm at liberty to say."

"There are FIG members in Souris?" Tibby Rose asked, astonished.

"In Souris *and* in Shetlock," the old mouse replied. "Every nation has its good and bad. There are those in Souris who detest their ruler's oppression of a smaller country, and there are those in Shetlock who are ashamed by their government's refusal to intervene. Indeed," he continued, "Shetlock's policy of turning a blind eye might be their undoing if they're not careful. . . . "

At first Alistair didn't understand what Uncle Silas meant, but then it struck him. "A Greater Gerander would mean no more Shetlock. Do you mean Souris might invade Shetlock too?"

"Clever lad," said the old mouse with a shadow of a smile. "That's a question all Shetlockers should be asking themselves, in my opinion. If they won't help Gerander for the sake of justice, they might at least consider helping us in order to save their own skins." He took a deep breath, then began to cough violently, both arms wrapped around his bony chest. It was several minutes before he was able to speak again.

"You should rest," Tibby Rose said softly.

"I will never rest until Zanzibar is king," the old mouse muttered, as if to himself. Then he sagged. "But you are right. I have an arduous journey ahead of me, and I will need my strength."

He lay back and pulled the ragged blanket up to his chin. Alistair, too, lay back, deep in thought. Could he really be Gerandan? It would certainly explain his ginger fur. But then why had no one in the family ever mentioned it? Too dangerous, perhaps. And then, even though he had a hundred questions buzzing in his brain, and it was only the middle of the afternoon, he fell asleep.

When he woke a couple of hours later, the old Gerandan was gone. Tibby was standing in the doorway of the shed, looking out. The rain clouds had vanished, and a hot sun beat down.

"Hey, Tibby, where's Uncle Silas?"

Tibby turned. "Welcome back, sleepyhead." Then she shrugged. "I don't know. I dropped off as well, and he'd already left when I woke up a few minutes ago."

Alistair stood up and brushed the dirt from his fur. "What do you think? Should we try to walk a bit farther before the sun goes down?"

"Sure," said Tibby, and after they'd both drunk from the trough of cool, clear water, they set off. They were skirting around the foothills at the edge of the Eugenian mountain range now, and the winding road was hilly with little shade. It was hard going, but after their experiences on the river Alistair was quite pleased to be on dry land again.

As they walked, he and Tibby talked over what the old mouse had told them.

"Imagine what it would be like to have your country invaded like Gerander was," said Alistair. "It must be terrifying to have someone just take over your home like that. Your home is meant to be the place where you feel safe." He shook his head. "It's just *not right*," he declared. "I don't understand how it could be allowed to happen."

"Me either," Tibby said. "But it's kind of like what's happening to us now, when you think about it. I thought Souris was my home, but if the Queen's Guards catch us they could lock us up for being Gerandan spies, though we didn't even know we were Gerandan. And we're completely powerless to stop them! But, Alistair," she added, "do you realize that if you're ginger and I'm ginger, it means we're both descended from Queen Cornolia's ginger child. So really, we're kind of like cousins, way back and—what's that?"

A shadow had fallen over them. Alistair looked up, expecting to see a cloud skittering across the sun. Instead, he was alarmed to see a giant owl looming above them. It was so close Alistair could see its eyes glittering like beads, its sharp beak quivering in anticipation. He knew he should run, should scream, but, as if trapped in a nightmare, Alistair stood frozen, his legs rooted to the spot, his cry of warning stuck in his throat.

"Ginger mouse!" the owl squawked. "Ginger mouse!"

Then it dived toward them.

15

The Three Sheets Tavern

A lice and Alex jogged through the dark for the next few hours, pausing often to listen for voices and footsteps behind them. But they heard nothing.

The sun was well and truly up by the time the exhausted pair reached the coast. The fishing boats had returned with their catch, and as they entered the outskirts of Shambles, they saw a dozen or so mice heading in the opposite direction, pushing carts stacked with crates of fish, bound for nearby towns and villages. Drawing closer to the port, they could hear the cries of the stallholders at the market that spread around the quay and into the streets of the old town.

"Shambles' shellfish, get it 'ere! All yer oysters, cockles like the clappers, wee willie winkles, and the mostest mussels. Shellfish alive-o!"

"Freddo's fresh fish! Come to Freddo's for your fill of the freshest!"

The fishermen were perched on the sea wall, untangling nets or mending them and watching the action of the market, while all along the quay shopkeepers were sweeping down the pavement and arranging their wares, and restaurateurs were putting out chairs and tables under striped awnings.

Alice and Alex skirted around the edge of the crowd of early risers who were clustered around the stalls. Alice peered up at every awning and shingle they passed, looking for the Three Sheets Tavern.

It was Alex who spotted it. "There!" Down a dark alley off the port was a rather battered old shingle with the words THREE SHEETS TAVERN inscribed on it.

Alex pushed open the heavy door into the tavern and Alice followed. Dust motes drifted in the sun rays that streamed through the window. Alex dropped the rucksack from his back with a groan of relief.

A big old wooden bar stretched down the right-hand side, while to their left was a line of cozy booths underneath the windows, and a scattering of tables and chairs in between. What struck Alice first was how quiet it was. No one stood behind the bar, and apart from a couple of customers sitting at a table toward the back, the tavern was empty.

"Excuse me?" Alice called into the silence. "Hello?"

The two customers at the back looked over, and Alice let out a piercing scream.

It was Sophia and Horace!

She staggered backward into Alex, who was staring at the silver-gray and coal-black apparitions open-mouthed.

"Alex, run!" Alice cried.

They turned, only to find the doorway blocked by two smoky gray mice.

Trapped between the two pairs of mice, Alice cast around desperately for another exit, but she couldn't see one.

"Julius!" she shouted. "Augustus! Help!"

"Help *you*?" said one of the smoky gray mice by the door.

"I don't think so," said the other.

Alice gaped at them. "You mean you're . . . ?"

"Julius," said the tall, thin mouse with a nose that turned down.

"Augustus," said the other, who was short and stout with a nose that turned up. "We don't help spies."

"Spies?" Alex bellowed. "We're not the spies—they

are!" He pointed an accusing finger at Sophia and Horace. "They pretended they were from FIG and they—"

"You see?" said Sophia, tilting her head to one side and looking at Julius and Augustus with wide, innocent eyes. "It's just as I said. Next they'll try to convince you that they're Alex and Alice, the nephew and niece of our dear friends Beezer and Ebenezer."

"But we *are* Alex and Alice!" Alice broke in.

"Isn't it just too awful of those evil Sourians," Sophia continued, as if Alice hadn't spoken. "They're even embroiling children in their fiendish plots! That's why we must find dear little Alistair before they do. You will help us, won't you?" Her face was a picture of concern. "Why, if they harm a single hair on his ginger head, I'll...I'll..." She broke off and Horace handed her a small white handkerchief with which she proceeded to dab her eyes. Alice had to admit it was a masterful performance.

"You—you...!" Alex, incoherent with rage, stormed toward her, but before he had gone more than a couple of paces Julius had caught him by one arm and Augustus by the other.

"Don't even think about it," snarled Julius as Alex struggled to free himself.

"Wait!" said Alice. "We can prove who we are. We have a letter for you written by our Aunt Beezer."

"Oh yeah?" said Augustus. "Let's see it."

Alice dropped to the floor and opened the front pocket of the rucksack. The note wasn't there! Maybe she'd put it in the main part of the bag? Quickly she unbuckled the straps, lifted out the heavy half-wheel of cheese and rummaged through the bag's contents. Nothing. Where could it . . . ? She lifted her head to look at Sophia, who gazed back serenely. Of course. That was why Sophia had insisted that Horace carry their bag to their room at the Riverside Inn: so he could search it.

She looked up at Alex, who was still being held by Julius and Augustus.

"They've stolen the letter," she said dully.

"Gentlemen, I'm so sorry to inconvenience you like this. Indeed, if dear Beezer hadn't assured me I could rely on you I certainly never would have troubled you."

"It's no bother at all, Sophia," Julius told her. "We're happy we could help."

"Any friend of Beezer's is a friend of ours," Augustus added.

"Now, if you just had somewhere we could lock them up for a few hours? I need to find a ship sailing to Souris tonight so I can deliver these two into the captain's keeping. I know they're wicked"—she shook her head sorrowfully—"but they're only children. I think the best thing to do is return them home."

Julius raised his eyebrows at Augustus, who nodded. "The cellar," they said in unison.

Augustus began to drag Alex toward the bar, and Julius grabbed Alice by the arm and followed.

"What about our rucksack?" Alice protested.

"Leave it," snapped Julius.

On the other side of the bar was a trapdoor, which Augustus opened to reveal a set of stairs leading into darkness. Julius gave her a push and Alice stumbled down the stairs behind her brother. The trapdoor slammed shut above them, and they were alone.

Alice stood in the pitch black, the smell of cold stone filling her nostrils. She felt completely helpless and hopeless. She couldn't even see her brother. "Alex?"

"Here," said a voice to her right. "Ouch!"

"What's wrong?" asked Alice, worried.

"I've just banged into something." Alice heard a tapping sound and then Alex said, "This wall's just got empty wooden crates stacked in front of it."

"What are you doing?" asked Alice.

"Looking for another door," said Alex impatiently. "Come on, give me a hand."

"Oh, good idea." Alice stepped forward tentatively, arms outstretched. She took a second step, then another and another, then, "Ouch!" She had grazed her fingers on the rough stone of the cellar's back wall. Cautiously she felt along it, moving to the left corner, then the right. "Nothing here," she reported. "Just stone."

Alex, who had worked his way along the opposite wall, under the wooden staircase, said, "A couple of empty barrels over here. No door though." He sighed heavily.

Alice slumped to the dirt floor and put her head in her hands. "Oh, why did we ever leave Smiggins?" she sobbed. "Uncle Ebenezer was right: it was too dangerous. Now we'll never see Alistair again, and we don't even know what's happened to him. And Uncle Ebenezer and Aunt Beezer will never know what's happened to us, and . . ."

Then Alex was at her side. "Come on, sis. Don't go to pieces on me now. We're not dead yet, are we? And as long as we're still alive we've got a chance."

Alice straightened and wiped her eyes with her hands. "You're right." She sniffed. "Maybe they really will take us on a ship? We could jump overboard—we're both strong swimmers."

"That's the spirit," said Alex.

They passed the time remembering some of Uncle Ebenezer's most daring escapades and imagining themselves performing their uncle's daring feats.

"We could climb a tree," said Alex.

"And when they came after us, we could somersault

off it," said Alice. She was starting to feel better now. What was it Aunt Beezer had said? They were brave, resourceful, and capable, that was it. Well, if there was ever a time to be brave, resourceful, and capable, it was now. She felt for her brother's hand in the dark and gave it a squeeze. "Thanks, Alex," she said.

Alex returned the squeeze briefly and then snatched his hand back. "Of course, it's easy to somersault out of a tree," he said. "Unless you're holding another mouse by the tail."

They were giggling as the trapdoor was suddenly flung open and light spilled down the stairs. There was a scuffle, and Alice heard Horace say, "Please don't make me go down there, Sophia. I don't like cellars," and Sophia respond, "Oh, very well, Horace—it seems I must do *everything* myself."

Blinking, Alice peered up the stairs at the figure silhouetted against the glare.

"So glad to see you're having fun," Sophia said. As her eyes adjusted, Alice saw that she wore an acid expression. "Enjoy yourselves while you still can, won't you?"

Alice felt all her earlier bravado drain away, leaving her timid and scared, but still curiosity compelled her to ask: "How did you—?"

A brief cold smile flashed across Sophia's face. "Get

here so fast?" she said. "Boat. Really, dear, we'd get along much better if you just accepted the fact that I will always be a step ahead of you." She shook her head. "Anyway, Tweedledum and Tweedledee upstairs seem to think we're obliged to feed you." Without ceremony, she dropped two bread rolls into the dirt at the foot of the stairs. "Your last meal," she said. "I do hope you find it to your liking."

Then the trapdoor was slammed shut, and Alice and her brother were plunged back into darkness once more. They slowly felt their way across the ground on their hands and knees, trying to find where the bread rolls had fallen.

"Got them," said Alex after a couple of minutes. It never took him long to find food.

He handed one of the rolls to Alice and she carefully brushed the dirt from it. Sophia's reference to their impending death had not done much for her appetite, but she knew she needed to keep her strength up.

"Cheese and sardine, not bad," said Alex. "Though not as inventive as Uncle Ebenezer's sandwiches—blue cheese and tuna, yum. Still, thoughtful of Julius and Augustus. They must be all right, really."

"I'm sure they are," said Alice, who was finding the pungent little fish a bit, well, *fishy* for her liking. "After all, they think we're Sourian spies out to get Alistair.

We can hardly blame them for throwing us in the cellar. And they're not the first people to be fooled by Sophia, are they?" She looked at her brother meaningfully, but since it was too dark to see meaningful looks, Alex was oblivious.

"If only there was a way to convince them that we are who we say we are," mused Alex.

"There's no need."

"What?" Alex started. "What's wrong with your voice, sis?"

"That wasn't my voice, Alex," said Alice, who had sprung to her feet. "Who said that?" She looked around wildly, frustrated by her inability to see.

"Me . . . Julius." There was a sound of crates creaking and shifting, then they could just make out a tall, thin mouse standing beside them.

The two young mice gaped at him.

"Where did you come from?" said Alex. "We couldn't find another way out."

"There's an old smuggler's tunnel which comes out in one of the crates," the tall mouse explained. "Quick. We don't have much time. Horace is upstairs with Augustus watching the trapdoor, and Sophia's gone out to meet the ship's captain she mentioned earlier."

"But what are you doing here?" asked Alice, confused, as hope began to dawn. "Why are you helping us?"

"Augustus and I had our suspicions about Sophia from the start," Julius confessed as he squeezed through a narrow gap between two stacks of crates, then folded his long thin body into a crouch, and crawled into a crate at the bottom of a stack against the wall.

"For a start, there's no way Beezer would have sent strangers to us without going through the regular channels. She's very cautious is Beezer. And then there was your rucksack. When I was moving it, I noticed an old label with your name, Alex, and the crest of Smiggins Public School. I doubt if even the most experienced Sourian spy would have bothered to find out what the Smiggins Public School crest looks like and sew it into a schoolbag. I only know it because Augustus and I went to Smiggins Public School ourselves."

"You did?" They were crawling through a close, damp tunnel now, so low that Alice couldn't lift her head to see in front of her. She could hear Alex breathing heavily behind her.

"I was in the same class as Beezer," said Julius. "And Augustus was in the year below."

Alice was glad that he had kept talking. It took her mind off the feeling of walls closing in, off the slimy moss that coated the walls the further into the tunnel they went.

"Almost there," said Julius as the earth beneath their

hands and knees became damp and sandy.

Within a few minutes, they were crawling out of the tunnel into a clump of dense thorny shrubs. Alice pushed her way through the unforgiving shrubbery and onto a path sitting a little way above a small deserted cove enclosed by high cliffs.

"Thank you so much," she began, but Julius waved away her gratitude.

"You're not safe here. I imagine Sophia will be furious when she discovers you've escaped, and if she should catch you again . . . " He let the sentence hang and once again Alice remembered Sophia's silvery voice saying, *We'll get rid of them. Permanently.*

"You should get back to Smiggins as fast as you can," Julius advised.

"But Alistair——," Alex protested.

"We'll be on the lookout for Alistair," Julius promised. "Not much happens in Shambles without us hearing about it. If anyone has seen your brother, we'll soon know. I'm sorry I can't give you back your rucksack, but it would be a dead giveaway that I helped you escape. I told Horace I was going out to buy some more sardines, so I'd better go buy them and get back to the tavern. I want to be there to act surprised when Sophia returns and finds out you've gone. She thinks she's outsmarted us by pretending to be from FIG, but two can play that game. I'll let her think she's got us fooled, but I'm going to send a message to some FIG members in Souris suggesting they arrange to 'accidentally' meet up with Horace and Sophia while masquerading as Sourian agents. Then let's see how much information our side can trick out of that despicable pair." He smiled briefly. "You two wait till I'm out of sight, then follow this path up to that cliff. Where the path divides, you go straight ahead—it joins up with the coast road eventually. I'll be taking the right-hand fork back into town." He shook them each by the hand solemnly and wished them luck, then hurried up the path.

As Alice watched him go, she wished she could call out her thanks; Julius had pressed a small wad of money into her hand as he shook it.

When they could no longer see Julius on the path, Alice and Alex set off at a run.

"Woohoo!" said Alex, who was leading the way. "That was close, sis. But I told you Julius and Augustus were all right."

Alice, almost giddy with relief, refrained from pointing out that he had once thought the same thing about Sophia.

When they reached the top of the path, they paused to get their bearings. They were standing on top of a rocky headland, which jutted out over a cobalt sea. A smaller cliff crouched at the other end of the small cove they had just ascended from, and beyond that cliff Alice could just make out the bright colors of the Shambles port, glowing in the sun. Turning her head, she saw a rocky coastline of coves and cliffs stretching away to the east.

"That must be the path there," said Alex, pointing to a dirt track snaking away through the low scrub of rosemary, thyme, and gorse. There was no one around except for a lone figure in sunglasses further up the path, leaning against a rock and basking in the sun.

"That's not Julius, is it?" said Alice as they started along the path, squinting.

"Nah, too short."

But as they drew closer Alice's legs began to tremble so violently she almost fell over. It couldn't be . . .

"Sophia!" she croaked, her throat dry with fright.

The silvery gray mouse turned and regarded them through her sunglasses. If she was surprised to see the two mice she had so recently locked in a cellar now wandering along a clifftop, she didn't show it.

"Really, you two," she said. "Can't you stay where I put you for five minutes? I come up here for a nice private meeting with a colleague, and then you show up. It's hardly going to be a private meeting with you here, is it? I'm afraid you're starting to irritate me." She moved toward them menacingly. "And I'm not very pleasant when I'm irritated." She lifted a hand as if to scold them, and with a flash of terror, Alice realized that she was holding a knife.

"Alex . . ." But a quick glance at Alex's pale face told her that he had seen it too.

The two young mice backed away carefully as Sophia advanced, the knife's blade gleaming.

As they drew closer to the cliff's edge, Alice cast around desperately for an escape route. Sophia was blocking the path that would take them either to the coast road or back to Shambles. What about the cove? But she quickly discarded the idea. The cove was fully enclosed with no way out, other than . . . the tunnel? Looking back down the path, she could no longer tell which bush concealed the tunnel's mouth. Anyway, to lead Sophia to the tunnel would mean betraying Julius and Augustus. No. There was only one way of escape— though success was by no means certain.

"Alex," said Alice, swallowing hard. "What was it Uncle Ebenezer said about jumping off cliffs?"

Alex glanced over his shoulder and then looked at her questioningly. Alice gave a small, resigned nod.

"He said to close your eyes so you can't see how far you've got to fall."

That sounded to Alice like the most sensible advice Ebenezer had ever given them.

"Okay then," she said, taking a deep breath. "Let's do it."

And the two mice turned, ran, and leaped . . . straight off the cliff.

16

Resistance

Ginger mouse!"

As one of the giant hunter's talons closed around him Alistair screamed, "Run, Tibby!" But even as he spoke, the owl's second talon had snatched up his friend. After that, Alistair had no breath to scream, for the talon was wrapped around his body like a vice, and it was all he could do to breathe. He tried to turn his head to see Tibby Rose, but the owl's grip was too tight.

With a few beats of the owl's powerful wings, they were airborne, the ground far below a blur as they sped through the golden rays of the sun setting to their right. Alistair mostly kept his eyes closed, his thoughts full of trepidation, for surely the owl must soon reach its destination. Alistair was surprised that it hadn't killed and eaten them instantly. Perhaps it was taking them home to feed to its chicks? He began to wish that the owl *had* killed them instantly. Anything would be better than this horrible suspense. . . .

But as sunset turned to dusk and dusk to dark, Alistair began to wonder just where the owl was taking them. Surely owls didn't hunt so far from their own territory? Opening his eyes, which immediately began to water because of the wind, he tried to get some idea of where they were—no easy task considering his grasp of Sourian geography was based on a quick glimpse of a map in Great-Aunt Harriet's library and a diamond scratched in the dirt by the river's edge in Templeton. A tremor of fear and nausea racked his body as the owl banked to the left. Squinting at the dark land below, he saw a great cluster of lights. Could it be Grouch, all the way on the other side of the Eugenian Range? Could they really have flown so far?

They banked again, to the right this time, and the lights vanished beneath them. Alistair closed his eyes and thought of all the things he would miss in his life. Alice's quick mind and Alex's loyalty. Uncle Ebenezer's stories and Aunt Beezer's dry wit. He thought of Ms. Emily the librarian and Mr. Russo, his favorite teacher. Of Mrs. Zetland and her biscuits and Mr. Grudge's garden. Of his best friends at school, Linus and Betty. Then he thought of Tibby Rose, who had never known her parents, never had brothers and sisters or friends and neighbors, growing up alone in that big old house with her two elderly relatives. It was sad that her life was going to be cut short before she had ever really lived.

Some time later, they banked once more and Alistair opened his eyes. The first thing he saw in the dark was the moon, and he felt disoriented. Why were they flying upside down? Then the moon rippled, and he realized it was a reflection, that they were flying over water. Then the moon disappeared, and they were soaring over a clifftop. For one terrible moment, Alistair thought that the owl might be planning to release them, and that they would be dashed against the rocks below. Maybe that would be preferable to being eaten? He didn't know; both options seemed too hideous to contemplate.

Then the owl hooted once, and they were coming in to land in a small clearing hidden among the dense coastal scrub. Suddenly the owl loosened its grip on Alistair's body and he was falling. . . .

"Where am I?" he asked as his fall was broken not by hard ground but by something furry and wriggly.

"On me," gasped Tibby Rose. "Haven't we been

through this before?"

Alistair had a flash of memory to when he and Tibby had first met. He had fallen—from nowhere it seemed. Was it possible . . . ?

Alistair jumped to his feet and turned to face the owl, who was standing nearby calmly grooming his feathers.

"It was you!" Alistair cried. "Wasn't it? I heard a tapping on the shutters in the middle of the night, and I opened them, and I think I must have bumped my head—and the next thing I knew I was in Templeton."

The great grave face stared back at him impassively.

"And you were calling 'ginger mouse' back there when neither of us are ginger anymore. Why?" Alistair demanded. "How did you know?"

"That would be our doing," said a voice behind him.

His heart racing, Alistair spun around to see the faint silhouettes of two mice.

"We asked Oswald to take you from Smiggins to Templeton, Alistair, and when Timmy the Winns told Oswald he'd seen you, Oswald told us. We asked him to find you and bring you here."

"Who—who are you?" Alistair stammered. "And how do you know my name?"

"Come closer," suggested a second voice, "and we'll explain. You too, Tibby Rose. I can barely see you in the dark."

As Alistair and Tibby Rose hesitated, the first voice spoke up again. "Don't worry—we won't hurt you. We have your best interests at heart, I can assure you."

A bit uneasily, Alistair edged forward, Tibby close beside him.

When they drew near, Alistair saw that the two mice were sitting before a fire that was burning so low it cast barely any light.

"Who are you?" he repeated.

The mouse who had first spoken stood up. He was tall and lean, with a shock of chestnut fur on his head and chest, while the rest of him was dark brown. "I'm Feast Thompson," he said. "It's a pleasure to meet you both."

"And I'm Slippers Pink," said the second mouse in a low, husky voice. Slippers Pink had beautiful pale almond fur and wore a pair of shiny black boots that went almost to her knees. "Come sit by the fire," she invited. "You must be feeling a little windswept."

Still stunned, Alistair and Tibby obeyed.

"There, isn't that better?" said Slippers Pink. "I love a good fire—even a small one." With a comfortable sigh, she pulled off first one boot, then the other, and stretched out her legs to wiggle her toes in the fire's glow.

Tibby gasped and clutched Alistair's arm. She was staring at Slippers Pink's feet. Alistair followed her gaze. The pale mouse's feet were a light gingery pink, almost the same shade as Tibby Rose's own natural color.

"Are you . . . Gerandan?" Tibby asked in a hushed voice.

Slippers Pink looked amused by Tibby Rose's serious tone.

"I was born there," she said. "Though I left when I was three and haven't been back since."

As Alistair and Tibby Rose gaped at her, Feast Thompson said, "We all have a lot of explaining to do— you two included." He looked at Alistair and Tibby Rose sternly. "I'd be interested to know exactly what you think you're doing wandering around the countryside when you should be safely tucked up in bed at Nelson and Harriet's house in Templeton. But"—he held up a hand to stop the protests of the younger mice—"we should eat first. I don't know about you two, but we're starving."

Alistair thought of Mags's cloth bag, still full of cheese and bread and strawberries, now at the bottom of the river. "Me too," he said.

Feast Thompson hooked a stick under the wire handle of a battered black pot that had been resting in the coals of the fire and lifted it onto the ground before him.

"We've not got much in the way of tableware," he said, as he handed around spoons. "We're traveling light. But dig in."

Alistair put a spoon into the light milky broth and carried it to his lips. It had a very unusual flavor, salty and briny, like nothing he had ever tasted before. He dipped his spoon in again and this time lifted out something solid. Well, sort of solid. When he put it in his mouth, it seemed to slither, then slid down in one slimy gollop before he even had a chance to bite into it.

"Ugh," he said in disgust. "What was that thing? It's like it was alive."

"You don't like oysters?" said Slippers Pink in surprise. "I suppose they are an acquired taste."

"What about you, Tibby Rose?" asked Feast Thompson.

"I like them," said Tibby Rose decidedly. "They taste like I imagine the sea would taste."

They kept eating—Alistair being careful to avoid the oysters and stick to the broth—until the pot was empty.

"So," said Feast Thompson at last, leaning back against a rock, "you've given us quite the run-around. Oswald couldn't believe it when he met with Timmy the Winns to exchange messages on another matter and Timmy told him he'd met you that very evening. Poor old Os had a devil of a time finding you. He wasted all last night patrolling up and down, and didn't see tail nor whisker of you."

"How do you know Timmy the Winns?" said Alistair. "And how did Timmy the Winns know us?"

"And how come you know Grandpa Nelson and Great-Aunt Harriet?" said Tibby Rose.

"Why take me to Templeton in the first place?" said Alistair.

"We didn't think anyone would look for you there," said Slippers Pink, answering the last question first.

"Look, it's very simple," Feast Thompson began.

"Well, not *that* simple, Feast," Slippers Pink objected.

"You're right," said Feast Thompson. "Actually, it's not simple at all. Alistair, your life was in danger, and we needed to get you to a safe place, somewhere no one would look for you. We had planned to take you there ourselves—in fact, we were on our way to Smiggins to fetch you—when there was a change of plan."

Alistair stared at Feast Thompson in bewilderment. "Why me?" he said. "I mean, why not Alex or Alice, for example?"

Feast and Slippers exchanged glances.

"Because you're ginger," Slippers said.

Alistair thought he was beginning to understand. "Is this something to do with Gerander?" he asked. Then another thought occurred to him. "Are you members of FIG?"

"What do you know about FIG?" the pale mouse asked sharply.

"It's a resistance movement fighting for Gerander's

freedom from Sourian occupation," Tibby Rose piped up.

"Who told you that?" Feast wanted to know.

"A . . . a mouse," said Tibby hesitantly.

Slippers swatted the air impatiently. "Of course it was a mouse," she said. "But which mouse? Hang on . . ." She turned to Alistair. "How much have Ebenezer and Beezer told you? They weren't supposed to tell you anything till you were older," she grumbled.

"Uncle Ebenezer and Aunt Beezer? They haven't told me any—wait, do you mean they're part of FIG too? But that's ridiculous; we're Shetlockers, not Gerandan."

"That's not entirely true," Feast Thompson told him. "Raskus—Rebus and Ebenezer's father—was Gerandan. And Emmeline was born in Gerander, and lived there for much of her childhood until she escaped."

Alistair sat with his mouth open, trying to take this all in. "So both my parents are Gerandan? I never knew." Suddenly he was bursting with questions. "Were they part of FIG? Did that have anything to do with how they died?"

"Slow down," said Feast. "I can only answer one question at a time. Yes, Emmeline and Rebus were part of FIG. As for your other question . . ." He shook his head. "I'm afraid so. They sneaked across the Gerandan border on what was meant to be a short mission and . . ." He let the sentence hang unfinished.

"They died on a mission?!" Alistair shouted. "What kind of mission?"

"Shhh," Slippers and Feast shushed him.

"For obvious reasons, we're trying to keep a low profile here," said Slippers. "So please do try to keep your voice down."

"But my parents," Alistair said through the lump that was building in his throat. "Where were they going? What were they doing? Why couldn't anyone save them?"

Slippers explained, "It's very hard to get information into, out of, and around Gerander, and very hard to travel within the country. The Sourian occupiers of Gerander keep watch on the mail, on all the roads—they're determined to prevent the citizens of Gerander from communicating with each other and organizing an uprising. But there is another way...." Slippers Pink tilted her head to one side as if appraising them. "Emmeline had special knowledge, you see."

"Slippers . . . ." Feast Thompson said in what sounded like a warning tone.

"It's okay," said Slippers Pink. "Timmy thought—" She stopped and turned to whisper something in Feast's ear. Then she turned back to Alistair and Tibby Rose. "What I am about to tell you is of the utmost secrecy," she said. "Do you understand?"

Alistair and Tibby Rose looked at each other and then nodded.

"And do you agree never to reveal this information?"

Alistair nodded again, though he wondered why he and Tibby Rose, who had never even heard of FIG and the history of Gerander's occupation until a few hours ago, should be entrusted with secret information.

Slippers continued, "There are other paths through Gerander. Paths known only to a few. They have never been recorded in writing, but are passed down through families in other ways; they are sung or painted or danced. If the secret of these paths was shared, it would mean members of FIG could travel freely through Gerander. And then, maybe, we could finally bring Gerandans together to rise up against the Sourian occupiers."

"And my mother?" said Alistair, who had an inkling of what was coming next.

"She knew the secret of the paths."

Slippers Pink looked at Alistair expectantly, but Alistair had no idea what it was she wanted from him. When it was clear she was finished, Alistair said, "So my parents . . . " He wasn't sure he could bear to hear the answer to his own question, but he had to know the truth. "So my parents were killed for the secret?"

Feast Thompson exhaled heavily. "We don't know.

Perhaps—though as far as we know General Ashwover and his army are unaware of the secret paths. It's more likely your parents were killed because they were identified as spies." His voice deepened. "I'm sorry, Alistair. But they knew the risks."

Alistair stared into the fire, struggling to come to terms with the idea of his mother as a spy, a spy with a special secret. . . .

"So where do I come in?" Tibby asked. "I suppose you're going to tell me that I'm Gerandan too."

"On your father's side," said Slippers.

"My father?" Tibby sat bolt upright. "You knew my father?"

Slippers said, "Yes, indeed: every member of FIG considers him a hero. And he wouldn't be pleased to know that you'd left your grandfather's house."

"So you knew I was there?"

"Certainly," said Slippers. "It was the safest place for you. And for Alistair. Though I'm afraid your grandfather and great-aunt must have been rather surprised to see Alistair. There was a . . . mishap."

Feast Thompson gave an embarrassed cough. "We had written them a note explaining Alistair's sudden appearance. Oswald was meant to leave it with them when he dropped you off but he, er, he swallowed it."

"But that doesn't change the fact that you never

should have taken off by yourselves," Slippers Pink said sternly. "Tibby Rose, your relatives made many sacrifices to keep you safe."

"I . . . I didn't know," said Tibby, looking ashamed. "I didn't know that they had to protect me because I was Gerandan. I thought they must be embarrassed by me because I was ginger."

"Not at all," said Feast Thompson. "They weren't happy about your parents' marriage, but only because they feared for Lucia's safety; they weren't at all bothered by the fact that your father was Gerandan. They're good people—and they must be beside themselves with worry about you now. I'm sure they'll be most relieved to see you when Oswald takes you back tonight."

"Takes us back?" said Alistair. "No. No way. I'm on my way home to Smiggins. My brother and sister'll be worried too, and my aunt and uncle."

Feast looked surprised. "Worried? They'll be glad you're safe. I'm sure our letter would have made it perfectly clear why it was necessary to remove you to Templeton at such short notice. But like I said, there was a change of plan. We have an urgent rendezvous near the Eugenian Range or we'd accompany you back to Templeton ourselves."

"But why can't Oswald take me back to Smiggins?" Alistair argued.

"Smiggins isn't safe for you," Slippers Pink explained. "One of our spies in the Sourian army learned that two of the Queen's agents were on their way to kidnap you."

"But why me?" Alistair asked for what seemed to him the fiftieth time. "I know I'm ginger, but if I'm Gerandan my brother and sister are too, so why is it only me that's in danger?"

He saw a strange look pass between Feast Thompson and Slippers Pink.

"Something's going on in Gerander at the moment," Feast said vaguely. "We're not sure what, but it's got everyone on the hop."

"Is it something to do with the prison break?" Tibby Rose asked. "And Zanzibar escaping?"

"Zanzibar—Zanzibar has escaped?" Slippers Pink gasped. She put a hand to her mouth and bowed her head.

"Are you sure?" Feast Thompson asked urgently. "How do you know?"

"The mouse I mentioned earlier...he told us. He told us about Gerander and FIG, and about how Zanzibar should be the king. He escaped from a prison in the Cranken Alps with Zanzibar. He said he was in Souris on an important mission."

"Our rendezvous," said Feast, almost to himself. He stood up and began to pace. "Right, we've got no time to lose. Slippers, let's go. Oswald, are you still there?"

There was a hoot from a tree at the edge of the clearing, then Oswald swooped down to join them.

"Wait," said Alistair. "Wouldn't it be quicker if Oswald took you to your rendezvous first, then came back for us?"

Slippers shook her head. "No, we're not leaving you here on your own. It's out of the question."

Feast looked at Slippers. "I don't know, Slips," he said. "The rendezvous... What if the Queen's Guards should reach him before we do?"

Slippers Pink looked torn. "But what if anything happened to Alistair and Tibby Rose?" she said. "It's a miracle we've found them again as it is. We can't take any more risks."

Feast Thompson shrugged. "It's your call," he said, "but at least we know where Alistair and Tibby Rose are now, and if they sit tight and wait here for Oswald, I can't see the problem."

"I guess," said Slippers Pink, still looking doubtful. Then she groaned. "But I wish we didn't have to fly, it makes me so queasy—no offense, Oswald."

"None taken," said Oswald in a deep voice.

Slippers pulled on her shiny black boots while Feast Thompson stowed the cooking pot in a rucksack that had been sitting in the shadows.

"You two wait right here till Oswald comes back for you," Slippers reminded them. Then she gave them each a hug and hurried to the center of the clearing. It looked almost as if she were crying, Alistair thought.

"It really was good to meet you both," Feast Thompson said, placing one hand on Alistair's shoulder and the other on Tibby's. "I hope that next time it's in happier circumstances."

He went to stand by Slippers Pink.

As Oswald's talons closed gently around them, Alistair heard Slippers say, "Oh, Feast, could it really be true? Could Zanzibar be free?"

Then with a flap of Oswald's mighty wings, they soared off into the night.

17

Ship Ahoy!

It felt to Alice like she was falling in slow motion, though in fact it was probably only a matter of seconds till she hit the water. She was momentarily stunned by the force of the impact, a sudden blow that knocked all the air from her body, then she was plunged into the sea's icy depths. The shock of cold brought her to her senses, and she swam for the surface, desperate for air.

She had no sooner broken the surface and taken a welcome breath, when she was pulled under again. Something had her by the tail! She struggled against it, kicking out, and finally wrenched free to take another gulp of air. Her tail was grabbed again, and this time she recognized the distorted shape beneath the waves as Alex.

"What are you doing?" she yelled at him as he surfaced beside her. "Let go! I need to breathe." Indeed, she was feeling rather short of breath, treading water in the large swell, trying to stay afloat.

"We can't let Sophia see that we survived the fall," her brother panted. "We need to get under the shadow of the cliff and then try to swim back to the cove."

Alice immediately saw the sense in what he was saying. If Sophia knew they were still alive, she would come after them; if she believed them drowned, they would finally be able to make good their escape. Alice took a deep breath and then, reluctantly, dived down into the icy water. The salt stung her open eyes, but she could just make out the shape of Alex ahead of her. She tried to hold the air in her lungs for as long as possible before letting it leak out slowly. She was starting to feel light-headed by the time she saw her brother swim up to the surface, and she kicked up to join him.

For a few seconds, neither of them could speak, all they could do was draw quick ragged breaths as they tried to stay afloat using as little energy as possible. When at last her heartbeat had slowed and she was able to look around, Alice realized that they had swum all the way around the cliff, and were now facing the small cove they had been heading toward.

Alex, who had been scanning the cliff, said, "I can't see any sign of Sophia. With any luck, she'll think we've drowned. All right, sis, final stretch—see you on the beach." And he set off toward the sand with a fast freestyle.

Alice, who was so exhausted she could barely move her arms, tried a more sedate breaststroke—after all, if Sophia was no longer after them there was no need to hurry, she reasoned. But it seemed that although she swam with all her remaining strength, she wasn't getting any closer to shore. In fact, she noted with alarm, she was getting *farther away* from shore!

"Alex!" she cried. "Alex, help! I'm being pulled out to sea!"

"Me too," her brother called. "The current's too strong." Turning, he swam back toward Alice. "Don't fight it, sis," he advised, "you'll only wear yourself out. If we can just stay afloat, we're bound to be picked up by a boat."

"I don't know if I can," Alice whimpered. "My arms are so tired."

"You have to, Alice," said her brother firmly. "Anyway," he said, mimicking Uncle Ebenezer, "staying afloat is the easy bit—try doing it when you're holding another mouse by the tail."

Alice laughed weakly, and kept paddling.

For a while her arms and legs seemed to move of their own accord, as if they no longer belonged to her, while she concentrated on keeping her nose above the choppy waves. But as time passed—it could have been minutes or hours, she could no longer tell, it just felt like they had been in the sea forever—her muscles began to ache and she became painfully aware of her limbs. If it wasn't for Alex, constantly exhorting her to keep going, reminding her that Alistair needed them, that Aunt Beezer and Uncle Ebenezer too might be in danger, she was sure she would have given up, so great was her fatigue.

To her left she could still see the shore, but it was far away and getting farther. Even if the current hadn't been sweeping them on relentlessly, she doubted she could swim that far. What had she said earlier, in the cellar, about them being strong swimmers? She didn't feel strong at all; she felt very, very weak. Weak and tired. Oh, if only she could rest her weary arms and legs for just one minute, and rest her weary eyes as well. . . . That was better. So peaceful, dreaming and drifting. She felt wonderfully relaxed and . . .

"ALICE!"

Alice opened her eyes with a start. She took a breath and water filled her mouth and nose and she began to cough. Seized with panic, her mind went blank and she forgot how to swim, her arms lashing out wildly. And then she was floating on her back, and Alex was holding her beneath the chin, saying, "It's okay, sis, I've got you. Just stay calm."

After a few minutes her panic subsided. "I'm—I'm all right now," Alice said, and started to move her arms and legs with renewed determination. She was so ashamed of herself; her brother, swimming for his own life, had had to expend precious energy to save hers.

A breeze sprang up, sending clouds scudding across the sun, and the water grew cold.

"L-l-look," Alex said suddenly through chattering teeth. It was a ship!

"Help!" they called. "Help!"

But their voices were lost in the slap of waves against the ship's hull and the creaking of the rigging as the sails caught the breeze. Meanwhile, the wash of the ship's wake was sweeping them farther from their goal.

"HELP!"

Then a voice rang out: "Captain, there's two mice on the starboard bow!"

"What are they doing there?" a gruff voice demanded.

"Drowning, I think," said the first voice. "What should we do?"

"What should we do?! Throw 'em a line and pull 'em in, son—and be quick about it!"

A lifeline was thrown and the two young mice clung to it desperately. As they reached the ship's hull, a rope ladder was lowered.

"You first, sis," said Alex, and Alice began to climb, her weak muscles and frozen limbs screaming in protest. As the ladder lurched and swung with the movement of the ship, it was all Alice could do to hang on. Then hands were reaching down to help her over the rail and she was safe on the deck. She stood for a moment, swaying on unsteady legs, then everything went black, and she collapsed.

When she opened her eyes she saw a circle of concerned faces, the most worried of which belonged to Alex. He had a blanket wrapped around him, and when she lifted her head, Alice saw that she too was covered.

"Poor wee thing is just exhausted," said a shaggy brown mouse. Alice recognized the gruff voice as the captain's.

As she sat up slowly, Alex turned to the captain and said, "Please, sir, can you take us back to Shambles? We're needed at home—urgently!"

"Well now," said the captain, regarding the two shivering mice on his deck with a kind look. "Let's go down to my cabin and discuss it. I'll get Cookie to rustle up some hot chocolate."

Alice and Alex followed the captain down the stairs, Alice stepping cautiously as she still felt unsteady on her feet. The captain led them along a short passage, then pushed open the door to his cabin.

Alice, entering the cabin last, heard the bell-like voice before she saw the familiar flash of silver-gray fur. There, sitting behind the captain's desk, was Sophia.

"Ah, I see you've found our two runaways. Thank you, Captain, dear."

And for the second time in ten minutes, Alice fainted.

When she woke up, Alice was no longer wrapped in a blanket. Instead, she was lying on the hard floor of the captain's cabin, bound at the wrists and ankles by thick rope, a gag stuffed in her mouth. Alex, similarly trussed up, was beside her. All they could do was stare at each other wide-eyed as the conversation went on around them.

"I'm sick of the sight of them," Sophia was saying. "Put them somewhere I won't have to look at the little brats while I try to decide what to do with them."

"Are we going to take them to Souris, Sophia?" It was Horace's mournful voice.

"Maybe, Horace. Or we might just drop them overboard."

The captain, who no longer seemed so kindly, bellowed

for his cabin boy. "Get two of the crew down here to deal with these enemies of Shetlock."

A few minutes, later the cabin boy returned with two beefy sailors. Alice tried desperately to signal to them with her eyes that she and Alex were innocent, and that Horace and Sophia were the enemies of Shetlock.

"This one's got a funny squint," said the taller of the two sailors as he dragged Alice out of the room by her tail. "Do you think that's because she's a spy?" As Alice wriggled in pain and protest, he gave her tail a sharp tug. "We should've let you drown," he said.

"Nah, this way'll be more fun," said the other sailor, who had hold of Alex's tail. "We'll get to *enjoy* watching 'em drown."

"Where are we meant to put them?" asked the first.

"Dunno, the captain just said to get 'em out of sight. Hey, how about in there?"

And so Alice and Alex found themselves deposited unceremoniously in a barrel under the stairs, unable to speak or move, to await their fate.

If only, Alice thought dully, the barrel didn't smell quite so strongly of pickled herring.

18

The *Sickert*

When the giant bird bearing Feast Thompson and Slippers Pink had disappeared from view, Alistair and Tibby Rose settled down to wait. Alistair felt rather deflated. After all their adventures, all the narrow escapes and near misses and clever plans, it turned out there was no need to have undertaken the journey at all: he was meant to be in Templeton. And far from missing him, his aunt and uncle had known he was there all along. Alistair supposed they would have explained his sudden disappearance to Alice and Alex by now—though it would have been nice if they'd taken the time to explain to Alistair himself that he was going to be snatched by an owl and flown to another country. Indeed, why hadn't they told him? He wouldn't have objected if they'd explained to him why it was necessary.

The more he thought about it, the more it seemed to him that his aunt and uncle couldn't have known. Was it possible Oswald had swallowed that letter too? And anyway, just because Slippers and Feast (and maybe Ebenezer and Beezer) had decided that he was best off in Templeton, what about what he wanted? No one had bothered to ask him. He remembered what Tibby had said about taking risks and living your own life. It seemed to him that was exactly what his parents had done. They had risked their lives fighting for something they believed in. And as hard as it had been for those they had left behind, Alistair could now see they had been fighting for something that was worth more to them than their own lives: the freedom of all Gerandans. They had obviously decided they couldn't just sit back and do nothing. But what kind of life would *his* be, stuck in Templeton, even if he did have Tibby Rose for company? He turned to his friend.

"Tibby," he said, "I'm not waiting for Oswald to come back. I don't want to go to Templeton; I'm going home to Smiggins." He felt bad about disobeying Feast and Slippers. They were on the same side, after all, even if Alistair and Tibby Rose hadn't actually chosen to be on a side. But same side or not, Alistair couldn't imagine sitting quietly in Grandpa Nelson and Great-Aunt Harriet's big old white house on the hill outside Templeton (For how long? His whole life?) while others carried on the fight his parents had considered worth dying for. No. He might be only a kid, but he was part of this. He had almost been kidnapped, after all! (Though it seemed to him that Feast Thompson hadn't really explained why it was that Alistair alone was in danger, and not his brother and sister.) He would join FIG and help the resistance in any way he could. But first he had to see his brother and sister, his aunt and uncle. He had to know that they were safe, and reassure them that he was too.

Tibby, her head bowed in thought, walked slowly across the clearing to stand in front of the fire, which was now little more than a pile of glowing embers.

Probably she would be relieved to be reunited with her grandfather and great-aunt and resume her quiet, lonely but *safe* life in Templeton, Alistair supposed. He would be sorry to lose her company, though. In some ways, he felt closer to her than he did to Alice and Alex. Perhaps it was because of all the dangers they had faced together and overcome. Or maybe it was because they had so much in common—they both liked books and apple pie, and they both hated blackberries and being chased by the Queen's Guards. And they were both ginger.

At last Tibby said, "I feel terrible deserting Grandpa Nelson and Great-Aunt Harriet—especially now that I know how much they sacrificed for me. They have virtually lived in hiding themselves for all these years, just so I wouldn't be discovered. And yet..." Tibby sighed. "I don't want to live the rest of my life hidden away in Templeton. And not only that: if my father was Gerandan, then I am too. I don't want to be sheltered by FIG; I want to be part of it." It was as if she had read Alistair's mind.

Alistair couldn't help grinning, he was so pleased, but all he said was, "All right then, we'd better leave now. Oswald moves fast, so we haven't got long. And he'll be looking for us, so we'll need to stay under cover. That means we can't follow the path."

Tibby scooped up some sand and scattered it over the fire to put it out. "Let's go look along the coastline and get our bearings," she suggested.

They wound their way back through the scrub to the clifftop, and Tibby gazed left and right.

"There's a bit of a glow coming from over that way," she said, pointing to the west. "My guess is that's Sadiz."

"Sadiz?"

"It's a port."

"Great," said Alistair. "Let's go there. We can find a boat going to Shetlock."

They set off along the cliff, trying to stay under the shelter of the scraggly, stunted trees dotted through the scrub in the hope that would conceal them from the sharp-eyed owl.

"I just wish Feast and Slippers had told me more about my father," said Tibby as they walked. "I was only a few months old when he died, so I don't have any memory of him at all, and I've never met anyone who knew him—well, except for Grandpa Nelson and Great-Aunt Harriet, but they never talked about him at all. And they never even hinted that he was Gerandan."

"I guess it was just too dangerous," said Alistair. "Uncle Ebenezer and Aunt Beezer never told me. Gerandans seem to be really cautious about mentioning it to each other; there are probably spies on both sides. I mean, it turns out Timmy the Winns knew exactly who we were—I wonder how?—but he never so much as hinted at the fact that we were all Gerandan." Or had he? Alistair remembered what the midnight blue mouse had said about the River Winns: *It is the spine that knits our head to our feet. Its veins run through our country and its water runs through our veins.* At the time Alistair had assumed that when Timmy said "our" he meant himself and Griff and Mags and the rest. But was it possible that Timmy had been referring to himself and Alistair? He didn't know where the Winns was, but maybe it was in Gerander. He'd have to find out. He tugged the ends of his scarf thoughtfully. He still had a lot to learn about his homeland.

After spending the better part of two hours stumbling silently through the dark, they finally reached the headland overlooking the harbor town of Sadiz, which curved around a large calm bay. One end was dominated by a huge stone fort. Though it was too dark to make out the colors of the flag fluttering above it, Alistair thought it was a safe bet that they'd be purple and silver, the colors favored by Queen Eugenia. Below the fort, a fleet of fishing boats was anchored behind the protection of a sea wall. At the eastern edge of the port were the wharves where the big ships docked.

"Let's go down to the quay," said Alistair. "I've got a great idea."

"Shouldn't we wait till morning?" Tibby asked.

Alistair shook his head. "Nope. This is exactly the right time to find the kind of mice we're looking for."

"Insomniacs?" Tibby guessed.

"Pirates," said Alistair.

Tibby raised her hands to her ears and rubbed them vigorously. "Excuse me?" she said. "Did you just say *pirates?*"

"That's right," said Alistair. "That's my great idea: we're going to become pirates."

"Pirates," Tibby said again, as if she still couldn't quite believe what she was hearing.

"Feast and Slippers said that a couple of Sourian agents were looking for me," Alistair reminded her. "We don't want to come across one of them accidentally. So the important thing is anonymity, and that means we have to avoid getting stuck on a small boat with a chatty fisherman or the captain of a cargo ship who'll want to know who we are and might remember us later. A pirate ship is perfect. Pirates never want to know about your past."

"Alistair," Tibby said solemnly, "I'm worried about you. Are you feeling okay? Maybe a bit dizzy from our recent flight by Owl Airways? Light-headed from lack of sleep, perhaps? I've been relying on the fact that you are a thoughtful, careful, *sensible* mouse. But now we're heading to the roughest port in Souris, after midnight, looking for pirates."

Alistair laughed. "You know, you and Alice are going to get on like a house on fire. You're sounding more like her every day."

"I know you mean that as a compliment," said Tibby, "but I hope you won't be offended if I say that you're sounding more and more like your description of your brother Alex."

"Well," said Alistair, "they both used to tell me I should spend less time reading about adventures and more time having them. If only they could see me now!"

"If they could see you now, they'd tell you you're an idiot," Tibby said. "I doubt very much they meant you should actively seek out pirates."

"You might be right," Alistair said after a moment's reflection. "There weren't a lot of pirates in Smiggins. But do you have a better plan?"

Tibby had to admit that she didn't. "Okay," she said, "supposing for a minute that your idea is a good one— and I'm not saying it is—how would we even get aboard a pirate ship? We can't pay them, and surely stowing away is way too dangerous."

"Easy," said Alistair. "We join the crew."

"Oh, of course," said Tibby. "Why didn't I think of that?"

Alistair continued, "We find a pirate ship in need of a cabin boy and apply for the job."

"I see," said Tibby slowly. "So we're going to join a pirate crew. Interesting plan. I'm guessing there might be a book behind this?"

Alistair grinned. "*Treasure Island*. It's about this mouse called Jim Hawkins who becomes a cabin boy and meets a black-hearted pirate called Long John Silver."

"A black-hearted pirate, you say? Oh, that's excellent," said Tibby. "Do try your best to find a really black-hearted pirate captain to employ us, won't you, Alistair?"

They followed a winding path from the headland to the edge of town, then after a couple of wrong turns found themselves on a dark cobbled street that seemed to be heading in the right direction.

Although it was long past midnight, the port area was as lively as though it was midday. Light spilled from the tavern on the corner of the steep cobbled street where it met the quay, and they could hear the clink of glasses and cutlery, and the occasional voice raised in argument or song.

Alistair stopped and looked around. He saw warehouses interspersed with taverns, and the quay was busy with mice scurrying to and fro between the warehouses and ships, loading cargo.

Beckoning to Tibby to follow, Alistair slipped behind a dinghy leaning up against a warehouse wall to watch and listen. It was just as well they did, because suddenly a scuffle broke out between two mice, one brown and brawny and the other small and gray, who had just exited the nearest tavern.

After much shoving and shouting and flailing of fists, the gray mouse fell heavily against the dinghy they were hidden behind. He moaned once, then slumped to the ground, out cold.

The large mouse, looking a bit surprised to find an unconscious body at his feet, abruptly dropped the oar he had snatched up and scampered off, ducking up the nearest alley and out of sight.

"Is he dead?" came Tibby Rose's shocked voice in Alistair's ear.

"I don't know," said Alistair uncomfortably, peering around the edge of the dinghy, but then the mouse on the ground moaned, snorted, and began to snore. "Er, apparently not," he amended. He quickly pulled his head back to avoid being seen by three mice who were sauntering along the quay.

One of them nudged the sleeping mouse with his foot and laughed. "I wouldn't like to be the crew of the *Sickert* tonight," he said. "That's Captain Grizzard's cabin boy, and I don't think he's going to be ready to sail by first light."

"Grizzard?" said the portliest of the three, scanning the ships in the bay. "Is he docked tonight? I thought he was hanging around Shambles these days."

The mouse who had kicked the cabin boy pointed to a dark shape looming some way off and the other two squinted into the dark.

"He's up the end there—where no one can see what he's loading or unloading. They say he's just here for the night to take on new supplies before heading back to terrorize the cargo ships of Shetlock."

Alistair looked in the direction the mouse had pointed. Standing alone at the last wharf was a great wooden ship with two masts, its enormous sails billowing in the light breeze.

When the three sailors had disappeared into the Hoary Hornpipe, Alistair stepped out from the shadow of the dinghy. "Come on, Tibby. Here's our chance. This Captain Grizzard needs a cabin boy."

Tibby, looking reluctant, followed. "I don't see why I should have to be a cabin boy," she argued. "I'm a girl."

"But there were no cabin girls in *Treasure Island*," Alistair said. "In fact, I've never heard of a cabin girl."

"Oh, you've never heard of a cabin girl. . . . And you've been sailing the high seas for how long, Captain Alistair?" she said under her breath.

The lights and music faded as they walked toward the *Sickert*, and they could hear the slap of wavelets against the ship's bow, her timbers creaking as she rode the swell.

As they approached the gangplank, they were almost bowled over by a tall lean mouse who appeared to be departing the ship in a great hurry.

He was missing half of his left ear and he had a livid

scar stretching from his left temple almost to the tip of his nose. His eyes were small and close set, making the gaze he turned upon the two young mice seem suspicious.

"Whatcha doin' hangin' round'ere?" he demanded rudely. "If ya knows what's good for ya, you'll clear off sharpish."

Although inwardly he quailed at the mouse's harsh tone, Alistair addressed the sailor confidently. "Is your captain aboard?"

"Who wants t' know?" The sailor's tone was still disrespectful, but Alistair thought he detected a note of caution.

"That's Captain Grizzard's business and none of yours," Alistair told the older mouse calmly.

The sailor opened his mouth as if to retort, then clearly thought better of it. "He's in'is cabin," he said shortly, indicating with a thumb over his shoulder. "And ya'd better'ave good news for'im if ya value those long tails of yours."

As he turned to limp off toward the port Alistair and Tibby Rose noticed that he seemed to be missing a sizeable portion of his tail, which now barely reached the ground.

Tibby Rose gulped and clutched the end of her own tail protectively. "Do you—do you suppose Captain Grizzard did that?"

"If he did, I'm sure it's because the other mouse deserved it," Alistair said with more conviction than he felt. "Well, here goes..." And he strode up the gangplank with Tibby at his heels.

At first the ship seemed strangely deserted as they stepped onto the deck, but then Alistair saw that there were mice aboard, though they seemed to be doing their best to avoid drawing attention to themselves, scurrying noiselessly from shadow to shadow. The reason for their reticence was clear when a roar broke the silence.

"WHERE'S THAT SCURVY-LOVING, SQUID-RIDDEN, FISH-POCKED EXCUSE FOR A CABIN BOY?"

Alistair heard three sharp taps on the deck and then the owner of the voice stumped into view, his peg leg punctuating his progress. He was using his cutlass as a crutch, the metal blade buckling dangerously whenever the captain rested his not-inconsiderable weight on it.

His black fur was matted and patchy, one eye appeared to be permanently closed, and he had the longest, bushiest whiskers Alistair had ever seen. He clutched a telescope in his free hand and was muttering curses to himself. When he opened his mouth to shout at his cringing nut-brown first mate, Alistair saw the glint of gold teeth.

Tibby had just begun to whisper her doubts as to the

wisdom of his plan in Alistair's ear when the captain turned his one ferocious eye their way.

"WHO ARE YOU AND WHAT ARE YOU DOING ON MY SHIP?" he thundered, thumping his wooden leg on the deck to emphasize his rage.

Alistair was almost knocked backward by the powerful stench of onions. "Um, good evening, Captain, sir," he began hesitantly. He was beginning to doubt the wisdom of his plan himself. He only hoped Captain Grizzard would let them flee with their tails intact. "Ah, it's about your cabin boy. . . . Well you see, Captain, he appears to be indisposed, but, er, we are your new cabin boys. . . . ," Alistair swallowed, then finished in a rush, "So you will not be inconvenienced in any way."

"Actually," Tibby Rose said, "I'm a cabin girl."

"NEW CABIN BOYS?" the captain blustered. "CABIN GIRL?"

"Really," Tibby mused, "it makes more sense just to call us all 'cabin mice.'"

"CABIN MICE?" the captain repeated. He was regarding them with a slightly bewildered look. Then he seemed to recover himself.

"Well, let me tell you ROCKPOOL-REEKING, SARDINE-STINKING CABIN BOYS—er, cabin mice—how it's going to be. You will follow my orders EXACTLY and IMMEDIATELY or YOU WILL FEEL

THE LASH OF MY MOUSE-O'-SEVEN-TAILS!"

"Um, shouldn't that be a mouse-o'-nine-tails?" Alistair ventured.

Captain Grizzard lifted his upper lip to bare his golden teeth in a cruel smile. "Yes, it should, lad—and do you know what that means? I'm TWO TAILS SHORT!"

Alistair and Tibby Rose gasped, their hands flying instinctively to their tails.

"So mind you obey my orders, won't you?" the captain finished silkily. Then he turned and stumped across the deck and down the steps to his cabin, the smell of onions drifting in his wake.

The first mate looked at Alistair and Tibby Rose with a stony face which, as they watched, creased into a smile. "Welcome aboard, cabin mice," she said. "I'm Old Goosegob. Don't worry, me 'n' the crew'll look after you." She turned to address the figures lurking in the shadows. "It's all right then, lads, the captain's gone below."

With a murmur of relief, half a dozen rough-looking mice with shifty eyes, cunning noses, and crafty tails detached themselves from the shadows and gathered around the first mate for their orders.

"Right, you lot, let's finish loading those supplies then get ourselves a couple hours' kip. We sail at dawn."

"Excuse me, but what should we do?" asked Alistair,

but before Old Goosegob could answer there was a bellow from below decks.

"SHIP'S BOY!"

The first mate nodded in the direction of the stairs. "See what'is nibs wants."

Alistair and Tibby Rose hurried across the deck and down the stairs. They found themselves standing in a small corridor. From behind a closed door to their left, they could hear the distinctive tap-tap-tap of Captain Grizzard's wooden leg.

Alistair knocked on the door and then opened it. "Yes, Captain?" he asked.

The captain, who was seated behind an enormous mahogany desk covered with maps, greeted him with a blast of onion and abuse. "WHAT TOOK YOU SO LONG? When I call you I expect you to jump like jellyfish—ONLY FASTER! Have you got that?"

The two young mice saluted smartly. "Aye, aye, Captain!"

"Good. Now run down to the hold and fetch me an onion, and mind you're quick about it."

"Aye, aye, Captain!"

"Where's the hold?" Tibby Rose asked as they backed away from the cabin door.

"I have no idea," said Alistair. "But we'd better find it fast."

They ran down the corridor, past the stairs leading to the deck, and found themselves at the galley, face to face with a stout gray mouse in a grubby apron who was standing at a counter hacking oranges into pieces, rind and all, with a giant cleaver.

"What do you want?" he snarled, cleaver raised threateningly.

"Um, the hold, please," whispered Alistair.

"Downstairs." He dropped the cleaver into an orange. *Thump! Squelch.*

Alistair turned back toward the stairs, Tibby close behind him.

"Hurry," she urged. "The captain seems a bit impatient."

Down another flight of stairs they clattered, arriving at a long, low room, dimly lit with lanterns. It was half filled with barrels and crates of a most unusual assortment of things. There was a barrel of walking sticks, and another of umbrellas. One crate was piled high with hairbrushes, its neighbor with oven mitts. There were bow ties and silk flowers, sponges and gardening implements, and several bolts of cloth gaily printed with lollipops leaned against the wall. Alistair wasn't sure where Captain Grizzard kept his treasure, but it clearly wasn't in the hold.

After several long minutes, Tibby called, "Over

here," and pulled an onion from a barrel.

They pelted back up the stairs and along the corridor to the captain's cabin. It seemed that the sound of his wooden leg tapping on the floor was growing faster and louder by the second. Alistair had barely put his knuckles to the door when the captain yelled: "ENTER!"

The two young mice scurried into the cabin to find the captain glowering at them, brandishing a dagger.

Tibby let out a frightened squeak.

"The onion," the captain demanded, pointing to a spot on the desk with his dagger.

Alistair darted forward and put the onion on the desk, then quickly drew back.

The captain raised the dagger and plunged it into the onion then lifted it and, with a practiced hand, peeled it and took a bite.

"Delicious," he sighed, when he had finished crunching. "Now get back on deck and take orders from the first mate. AND NEXT TIME I NEED AN ONION, BE QUICKER ABOUT IT OR YOUR TAILS'LL BE FEELING THE SHARP EDGE OF THIS DAGGER!"

"Aye, aye, Captain!"

For the next two hours, Alistair and Tibby Rose were kept busy above decks and below. Tibby proved herself invaluable to the crew as a repairer of wobbly cart wheels, and the first mate put her to work with Scurvy

Smottle, the carpenter, while Alistair raced to and from the hold for Captain Grizzard, whose appetite for onions was insatiable.

Finally, Old Goosegob said, "Away then, lads, and grab yourselves forty winks afore the dawn."

Alistair and Tibby Rose followed the others down the stairs and past the galley to a series of berths furnished with hammocks and sea chests. The last berth, and the smallest, belonged to the cabin boy ("And girl," said Tibby). With some difficulty the two young mice clambered into the hammock and arranged themselves with Alistair's head at one end and Tibby's at the other.

At the sound of a bell clanging, Alistair sat bolt upright, making the hammock rock alarmingly.

Tibby Rose kicked him crossly. "What are you doing?" she said sleepily.

"I think it's time to get up," Alistair said, rubbing his eyes. He could see mice slipping out of hammocks, yawning and grumbling, and making briskly for the stairs.

He climbed out of the hammock and Tibby Rose, yawning and grumbling, followed. "You really do make an excellent pirate," Alistair told her.

As they filed past the galley, the stout, surly cook

handed each of them a slab of bread and a hunk of cheese.

The air on deck was fresh and cool with a pleasant salty tang, a welcome relief after the stale, stuffy air below decks. Standing at the rail as mice rushed around setting the sails and rigging, Alistair looked out over Sadiz, the sun tinting its square white buildings with gold. The great dome of the cathedral glowed yellow like the yolk of an egg. Despite the port's raucous nighttime revelries, the harbor was now a place of serious activity and industry. Along the wharves, voices echoed across the water as the crew from one ship taunted another. Captains and their mates bellowed orders, and the rigging of the ships lining the quay were alive with nimble mice. The fishing boats from the far side of the bay were returning to port with the day's catch, bobbing back to their moorings like little white corks with red and blue trim.

Captain Grizzard stood on the foredeck, shouting at any member of the crew who came within shouting range, while Old Goosegob stood at the aft issuing orders to the mice who scrambled about in the rigging. At a wink from the first mate the bo'sun cried, "Raise the anchor," and two strong mice heaved at a great iron chain. A gust of wind filled the sails and the *Sickert* began to move, slowly at first, then faster and faster till it seemed they were flying across the water. As they neared the mouth of the bay, Sadiz shrank behind them, until it resembled a small white stone gleaming on the shore. Tibby, who had been busy helping Scurvy Smottle, joined Alistair at the rail.

"Good-bye, Souris," she said, but she sounded quite cheerful.

Alistair turned to look at her, standing at the rail with the breeze in her browny purple fur and a smile on her face. "Tibby Rose," he said, "you look like you're *enjoying* being a pirate."

"Aye, Alistair, it's a pirate's life for me."

Alistair was taken aback. "But . . . but you're working alongside the most bloodthirsty mice on the Sourian Sea!"

Tibby shrugged. "They're not so bad when you get to know them."

"But what about Captain Grizzard? You have to admit he's terrifying."

"Oh, his squeak is worse than his bite."

"Squeak is worse than his bite?! He wants to cut off our tails! And he'd do it too—remember that mouse we saw when we first came aboard? He had hardly any tail left at all!"

"Oh, you mean Kipper?" said Tibby. "Apparently that was an accident. According to Smottle, Kipper was the ship's cook. He and the captain had a disagreement about the nutritional value of onions and Kipper stormed out.

Captain Grizzard slammed the door behind him and his tail got caught." She winced. "Ouch."

"Well, the rest of the crew seem scared of him," Alistair pointed out. "Look how they hang back when he comes on deck."

"They just don't like the onion fumes," Tibby explained. "It makes their eyes water."

At noon on their second day at sea, a cry rang out from the crow's nest.

"Ship ahoy!" called the lookout.

Captain Grizzard stumped to the side and held his spyglass to his good eye.

"Cargo ship," he declared.

"But what kind of cargo?" muttered Old Goosegob, who was at the wheel.

"Maybe it'll be gold," said Alistair, trying to sound enthusiastic and pirate-like.

Old Goosegob turned a glum eye on the cabin boy. "Captain Grizzard's not interested in gold, son. Nor jewels, nor pieces of eight, nor figgy biscuits, nor treasure of any kind." She snorted. "He's only interested in onions."

"Here's the plan," said the captain as he stumped over to join them. "We'll come alongside, then we board.

Down to the hold, plunder and so forth, bring the booty back here."

"Then we sink them?" asked Goosegob hopefully.

Captain Grizzard eyed the cargo ship speculatively. "Nah," he said. "Let 'em slink back to Shambles with their tails between their legs to haunt the taverns with tales of the fearsome Captain Grizzard."

"Hurrah!" cried Alistair impulsively. It sounded like the perfect plan to him—he and Tibby Rose could hide aboard the cargo ship and slink back to Shambles too.

Captain Grizzard glared at him fiercely. "I wasn't asking for your approval," he barked. "Now skedaddle down to the hold and fetch me an onion BEFORE I SLICE YOUR TAIL OFF!"

Alistair skedaddled.

19

Reunited

As the *Sickert* rammed the *Marmaduke* with a sickening crunch of timber, the pirates streamed across to the cargo ship with their cutlasses drawn. Alistair and Tibby Rose joined the throng.

"We should find somewhere to hide below decks," Alistair said to Tibby.

While some of the pirates stayed on deck to do battle with the *Marmaduke*'s sailors, another group scrambled down the stairs toward the hold.

Alistair and Tibby Rose scrambled after them.

As they reached the bottom step, Alistair said, "Follow me, Tib," and darted under the staircase. "Look, we can hide behind this barrel till we reach Shambles."

But Tibby, who was standing on tiptoes to peer into the barrel, said, "Alistair, I'm not so sure this is a safe hiding place. There's something in this barrel I think you should see."

"Pickled herrings, I presume." Alistair, waving a hand in front of his nose, joined Tibby Rose and peered into the dark container. But instead of pickled herrings, he saw two pairs of eyes staring back at him. Two familiar pairs of eyes. Surely it was impossible—and yet . . .

"Tibby, quick," said Alistair. "Help me lower the barrel to the ground!"

As gently as they could, they eased the barrel onto its side and pulled the two captive mice from it.

"Alice," cried Alex as soon as Alistair took the gag from his mouth, "there's a mouse here who looks just like Alistair—only . . . kind of purple."

"Thank you, Alex, I've got eyes," said Alice, whose gag had been removed by Tibby Rose.

"Alex," said Alistair, wrapping his arms around his brother's tied-up body, "it *is* me: Alistair. Oh, it's so good to see you both!"

"Alistair!" said Alex. "It's really you! Don't worry, we've come to rescue you!"

"That's a relief," said Tibby Rose drily. "Just give us a second to untie you and then you can get to it."

Alex's eyes flew to Tibby Rose, who was busy with the knots securing Alice. "Who are you? And why are you purple too?"

"It's a long story," said Alistair. "This is Tibby Rose— she's kind of a cousin of ours, in fact, and under the purple she's ginger, like me and... I'll explain later. More importantly, what are you doing here? And why were you tied up?"

"We were looking for you," said Alice. "We were hoping to find you before you were taken to Souris. But then Horace and Sophia—they're Sourian kidnappers— found us."

"Only they weren't actually kidnappers," Alex interrupted, "since they hadn't actually got you."

"But they were still kidnappers," Alice argued, "since they were *trying* to kidnap him—and they kidnapped us. Twice. Or is it three times?"

"True," Alex agreed as Alistair untied him. He rubbed his wrists where the rope had cut into them. "Three times if you count the Riverside Inn."

"That must be the pair of Sourian agents Feast Thompson and Slippers Pink were talking about," Alistair said to Tibby Rose. "Where are they now?" he asked his brother and sister.

"In the captain's cabin last time we saw them," said Alice.

"Then we'd better get off this ship before it docks at Shambles," said Alistair.

"Shambles? This ship sailed from Shambles," said Alice. "It's going to Souris."

"Not anymore," said Alistair. "Your ship was attacked by a pirate ship."

"*Our* pirate ship," Tibby Rose chimed in.

"You're pirates?" Alex said. He sounded confused. "Is that why you're purple?"

"No," said Tibby. "We're purple because we're ginger."

"I get it," said Alice. "And you didn't want anyone to know you're Gerandan."

"How do you . . . ?" Alistair began, looking at her in astonishment. Then, hearing footsteps, he shook his head. "There'll be time for this later. Right now we have to deal with the fact that we're not safe on this ship with the kidnappers aboard, and we don't want to go back to Souris on the *Sickert*. We need a third option."

"There's a lifeboat on the port bow," said Tibby Rose.

"Brilliant! Can you lead us to it, Tib?" Alistair asked.

"Sure." Tibby was about to step out from their hiding place when a shaggy brown mouse rushed down the stairs.

"That's the captain," whispered Alex.

All four mice peered around the corner of the stairs

to watch as the captain burst into his cabin.

"We're under attack," he announced to those inside in a hoarse voice. "Pirates. We can't fight them off, so we're going to turn about and head back to Shambles."

"P-p-pirates?" one of the cabin's occupants wailed. ("Horace," Alice whispered.)

"My dear Captain, that is completely unacceptable," came an imperious reply in silvery tones. "We are on our way to Souris." ("And Sophia," Alice added with a shiver.)

"I'm afraid that's impossible, Miss Sophia," said the captain, his tone hardening. "I must consider the safety of my crew and ship first. As it is we'll be lucky if the pirates don't scuttle us."

"Hmph. Very well." Sophia did not sound happy. "Then we had better divest ourselves of our young captives, Horace. We don't want those nasty Sourian spies setting foot on our precious Shetlock soil again. Where did your sailors put them, Captain?"

"In the barrel beneath the stairs. You can't miss it— just follow the smell of pickled herring."

"Yikes! Tibby, get us to that lifeboat," Alistair urged.

The four young mice scrambled up the narrow staircase.

On deck, the *Marmaduke*'s crew were fighting hard to repel the invaders. Fortunately, they were too busy to pay attention to the four young mice scurrying through their midst.

They were almost at the rail when they heard a screech from below decks.

"They're gone! The brats have gone!"

"Everyone over the rail!" shouted Alistair.

The four mice clambered over the rail just as Horace's lugubrious voice bayed, "There they are, Sophia!"

"Stop them!" the silvery mouse cried. "I order you sailors to stop them!"

But the *Marmaduke*'s sailors were too preoccupied fighting off the pirates to pay her any heed.

Casting a glance over his shoulder as he dropped down into the lifeboat, Alistair had a glimpse of silvery gray fur moving rapidly across the deck, pushing through the throng impatiently. A coal-black mouse trailed somewhat reluctantly in her wake.

"Tibby, how do we launch this thing?" Alistair asked urgently.

"It's lashed to the rail with rope," Tibby shouted. "We need to cut it." She looked around the bottom of the boat frantically.

Quick as a flash Alex was hauling himself back over the rail.

"Alex!" cried Alice. "Where are you going? Come back!" She tried to snatch at his tail but missed.

"Excuse me?" Alex tapped the shoulder of a pirate who was holding the point of his cutlass at the throat of a sailor whose back was pressed to the rail.

"What?" the pirate barked impatiently.

"I need your cutlass," said Alex, snatching it from the grasp of the bewildered pirate.

"Hey!" he shouted, but Alex took a running jump and, with one hand on the rail, hurdled back into the lifeboat.

"Here." He thrust the cutlass at Tibby Rose, who grasped the heavy sword with both hands and swung it through the ropes attaching the lifeboat to the ship.

"Hang on!" she cried, as the small boat fell several meters, hitting the water with an almighty splash.

Alistair, who was ready with the oars, began to stroke quickly away from the *Marmaduke*.

"Come back!" Sophia was shaking her fist from the deck above. But Sophia and the doleful Horace were the only mice aboard to pay any mind to the departure of the four young mice.

"Thank goodness you disguised your ginger fur," said Alice, watching with a mixture of terror and relief as the enraged silver mouse ran along the deck. "If she had known you were so close . . . " She shuddered.

Pulling hard at the oars, Alistair glanced to his left and right and over his shoulder but could see no sign of land. "Tibby," he asked, "which direction should I be rowing in?"

Tibby too looked all around, then she squinted at the sky. "That way." She pointed to her left, which was Alistair's right.

Alex and Alice gaped at her.

"How do you know?" asked Alex. "I mean, we're in the middle of the sea with no landmarks or map or anything."

"Tibby knows all kinds of amazing things," said Alistair, feeling rather proud of his new friend.

Tibby pointed at the sun. "Shetlock is south, and the sun sets in the west. Since it's early afternoon and I'm facing the sun, south must be to my left. But there's something else. See those white fluffy clouds? They're called cumulus clouds. If you see a group of them in an otherwise cloudless sky, they're usually sitting over land."

"Wow. That's a handy thing to know," said Alice as Alistair corrected course with the oars.

Tibby shrugged modestly. "Your brother's not the only one who likes to read," she said.

For the first hundred strokes, Alistair felt jubilant. He was with his brother and sister, and he would soon be in Shetlock. The adrenaline of their flight from the *Marmaduke* had given him a surge of energy, and his strokes were strong and swift. For it wasn't just Sophia and Horace they had escaped—they had left all their pursuers behind: the Sourians who hated them for being ginger, the Queen's Guards, even Oswald and Feast Thompson and Slippers Pink. His oars rippled through the water as easily as a breeze through silk.

By the second hundred strokes he had settled into a steady rhythm. He no longer had the sensation that he was gliding effortlessly, but they were making good progress. The two ships were now some distance away, and the cries of the fighting sailors were faint.

"Alistair," said Alice, "if you weren't kidnapped, why did you disappear like that? And how did you end up on a pirate ship?"

So it was as Alistair had suspected—his brother and sister didn't seem to have any knowledge of his disappearance. "Well, I heard a tap on the shutters. . . ." He proceeded to explain how he had been plucked from their bedroom window in Smiggins and deposited on Tibby Rose's front path in Templeton.

"He landed right on top of me!" Tibby added. Then, because Alistair was becoming breathless trying to row and talk at the same time, Tibby Rose started to recount everything that had happened to them since they followed Uncle Ebenezer into Templeton and discovered how very unpopular ginger mice were in Souris. When she reached the bit about their discussion with Feast Thompson and Slippers Pink (leaving out

Slippers's revelation about the secret paths of Gerander, of course), and how they had run off to Sadiz before Oswald returned for them and then got jobs aboard the *Sickert*, Alistair rested his oars for a moment. He had done over four hundred strokes and was starting to tire.

"We're both going to join FIG," he explained. "Tibby decided she didn't want to go back to Templeton, and she's Gerandan too, because of her father. What do you think? It would be great if the four of us joined together."

"Alistair, that's incredible," Alice exclaimed. Alex was gazing at his brother in awe.

"It is, isn't it? Tibby'll be like D'Artagnan joining Aramis, Porthos, and Athos, and the four of us will set off to—"

"Uh, I was with you till the dart and yarn joined the ram," said Alex.

"And what book would that be from, Alistair?" Tibby Rose demanded. Alice giggled at Tibby's long-suffering sigh.

"*The Three Musketeers*, of course. Aramis, Porthos, and Athos are the three musketeers, and then they're joined by a fourth, D'Artagnan, who—"

"Actually, Alistair," Alice interrupted, "I didn't mean it's amazing that Tibby is our fourth musketeer. Though it is wonderful," she added, smiling warmly at Tibby, who gave her a shy smile in return. "What I meant was . . . I mean, the raft and escaping from the Queen's Guards and almost going down a waterfall and joining a pirate crew. I never knew you were so brave!"

"Brave?" Alistair had to laugh. "I've been scared stiff and desperate to get home the whole time. And getting home was worth taking some risks for." Then his smile faded. "But I don't think we have a home anymore. We won't be safe in Smiggins." He sighed. "But at least we'll all be together. And maybe . . . maybe if we join FIG we can continue Mum and Dad's fight to free Gerander." He tugged at his scarf absentmindedly.

"I love the idea of being part of FIG, like Mum and Dad were," said Alice. "But I'm not sure how Aunt Beezer and Uncle Ebenezer would feel about it. Uncle Ebenezer said he gave up on FIG after Mum and Dad died. He even throws out the letters they send him without reading them."

That explained why his aunt and uncle had never told him he was going to Templeton—because they didn't know. Alistair was pleased that they hadn't hidden it from him. But it meant they would have been surprised and upset by his disappearance, as he had first feared.

Alistair picked up the oars and resumed rowing as Alice, helped by Alex (who didn't always agree with Alice's version of events), filled them in on their conversation with Aunt Beezer and Uncle Ebenezer the

270

morning they had discovered Alistair missing, and how they had learned all about FIG and Gerander and set off to find their brother.

As Alex and Alice's story unfolded, the other two were excited all over again by their fortunate meeting with Alistair and Tibby Rose on the *Marmaduke* and their escape from Horace and Sophia, but when the *Marmaduke* and the *Sickert* vanished over the horizon (six hundred strokes), Alistair's earlier euphoria vanished with it. With the sun beating down relentlessly, it was rapidly becoming clear to him what a foolish thing he had done. Here they were, in a tiny lifeboat in the middle of the sea. He had no idea how far from land they were or how long it would take them to get there. Why hadn't anyone stopped him? They had all seemed to think he knew what he was doing. But of course, he had no idea at all. . . .

By seven hundred strokes, the top of his head and the tips of his ears were burning. His neck itched under his scarf, the muscles in his arms were screaming and his back ached. Blisters were forming on his hands where he gripped the oars.

"That's it," he gasped. "I can't row any farther."

"I'll do it," Alex volunteered, and he and Alistair swapped places.

Alistair sat with his head in his hands, trying to shade himself from the sun's glare, while Alice and Tibby Rose talked quietly. From a few words he heard, he gathered that Tibby Rose was telling Alice about her parents, and how she had come to be living with her grandfather and great-aunt.

The afternoon wore on, and Alex was replaced on the oars by Tibby Rose and then Alice. Conversations about FIG and Gerander were replaced with desultory complaints about the brightness of the sun, their raging thirst, and gnawing hunger.

Hours passed and they seemed to get no closer to the clouds Tibby Rose had pointed out. By the time Alistair had had three turns on the oars, he was starting to despair—how long could they survive in the middle of the sea with no food or water or shelter?

Then Tibby, who had been scanning the sea as Alice rowed and Alex dreamed aloud of an ice-cold blue cheese and strawberry smoothie with plenty of pepper, suddenly said: "Look over there. Does that look like land?"

Hope leaping in his chest, Alistair squinted at the horizon. And squinted harder. "I can't tell," he said with a shrug. "It's so far away it just looks like a smudge to me."

But eventually the smudge on the horizon, an indistinct line of gray at first, gradually resolved itself into a muddle of cliffs and vegetation. Then Alistair caught sight of a jumble of red-tiled roofs spilling higgledy-piggledy down a steep green slope. Shambles! Alistair took over the oars and began to row with renewed vigor.

As they drew nearer, he could make out more details of the town. The row of uneven buildings lining the quay, rising two or three stories above the shop awnings, painted in vivid hues that caught the eye and held it: a tall, narrow lemon yellow building with a single line of pale blue shutters beside a large stately mustard structure with shutters of forest green and graceful wrought-iron balconies; a cheerful, slightly shabby salmon pink house with mauve shutters, geraniums blooming in the pots on the windowsills, stood cheek by jowl with a neat cream building trimmed in red. After the stark whites and cool grays of Souris, Alistair's heart lifted to see the warm colors of home.

His arm muscles were screaming by the time they landed on a small beach at the western edge of the port but he didn't care. He nimbly alighted, followed by Alice, Tibby Rose, and Alex.

"I never thought I'd be glad to see Shambles again," said Alice as they hurried along the quay. "But I am."

Alistair felt his spirits rising. He was in Shetlock! Suddenly, the rigors of the day were forgotten, and he was no longer tired. "Let's go home!"

20

Home

Alice and Alex led the way through Shambles, and soon they were on the road which would, eventually, lead them to Smiggins.

The sun was finally setting as they drew alongside the river Alice and Alex had followed in the dark. Half hidden behind a delicate line of mauve clouds, the sun was visible only as a golden glow tinged with orange then red, reflected sharp and bright in the rippling river. Stretching away into the distance on the other side of the road were neat rows of olive trees and almond trees, interspersed with golden fields separated by lines of tall cypresses. The sensation of the warm gentle breeze on his fur and the familiar scent of the flowers growing wild along the verge combined to awaken in Alistair a feeling of pure happiness.

They walked through the night, past the Riverside Inn (with a sniff from Alice) and past the point where the path over Mount Sharpnest diverged from the road (no one, not even Alex, suggested they take the shortcut). They walked through the next two days and nights as well, stopping to sleep when they could walk no longer, but never for more than a few hours at a time.

When they were hungry, they looked for nuts and berries, and Tibby would hunt for mushrooms. (Tibby was the only one who could tell the difference between a field mushroom and the similar-looking but poisonous Death Cap.) If it was nighttime, they would find a sheltered spot and gather dry leaves and grass for tinder and twigs for kindling, then Tibby Rose would start a fire burning while Alistair and his brother and sister looked for heavier sticks and branches with which to feed it.

Sometime after midnight on the third day, they reached Stubbins, and detoured through the sleeping streets to show Tibby Rose the house where they had lived with their parents.

Alistair moved away from the others to lean against the small picket fence. Gazing at the stone cottage, which was barely visible in the dark, he tugged at the ends of his scarf and remembered again his final glimpse of his mother. *Keep it safe and never lose it*, she had said as she gave him the scarf. And then, unbidden, the tune Timmy the Winns had played by the fire near Pamplemouse filled his head. Was this where he had heard it before? Was it a song of his mother's? He began to hum, and then suddenly he was remembering the words—not the words Timmy had sung, though.

"A burning tree
A rock of gold
A fracture in the mountain's fold,
In the sun's last rays when the shadows grow long
And the rustling reeds play the Winns's north song."

He was murmuring the words to himself when Tibby appeared at his elbow.

"Are you okay, Alistair?" she asked. "You look like you're a million miles away."

"I think I am, Tib," he said, still trying to put the pieces together in his mind. "Or thousands anyway." Remembering that Slippers Pink had warned them never to reveal the secret about his mother's special knowledge, he kept his voice low so his brother and sister wouldn't hear. "You remember Slippers told us about how my mother knew about the paths of Gerander? I think my mother might have sung one of those secret songs to me."

"Really?" Tibby sounded excited. "How do you know?"

Alistair described the song about the river that Timmy the Winns had played while she slept. "And I think I recognized the tune because my mother sang it to me the night before she went away," he finished. "I was just standing here thinking about that night, and suddenly the words of the song came to me." He sang them to her under his breath.

When he was finished, Tibby nodded thoughtfully. "A fracture in the mountain's fold . . . It could be a secret path, couldn't it? Though the rock of gold and burning tree sound a bit unlikely. They could be landmarks, I suppose—but how would we ever find them among all the rocks and trees in Gerander?"

Before they could puzzle any further, they were interrupted by Alice calling softly, "Alistair, Tibby Rose—we should set off soon if we want to reach Smiggins by dawn."

They walked back to the road to join the others.

"Four more hours and we'll be home," said Alex. "Hey, sis, remember how mad Horace was because he'd thought he'd only have to go from Smiggins to Stubbins to find us, and instead he ended up walking all the way to

Shambles?" He chuckled.

"But why would he think you were going to Stubbins?" Alistair asked.

"Hmm," said Alex. "Good question."

"There's something that I've never quite figured out," Alice said. "You see, Mr. Grudge said he'd seen a pair of mice, one gray and one black, standing beneath our window with a ladder. So of course when we first saw Horace and Sophia, we presumed they were the kidnappers. But if they *were* the kidnappers, how come they didn't know where you were? It turned out that they *had* come to kidnap you, but then Mr. Grudge must have chased them away. Of course, you were already gone by then, but they couldn't have known that, since they never got to climb the ladder—except they did know. That's why they were following us to get to you. . . . But they were surprised when we didn't know where you were."

Alice had stopped walking by this time, and was staring into the distance with a preoccupied expression. "Could it have been someone from FIG? A double agent?" She looked briefly alarmed, then murmured, "No, Uncle Ebenezer would have told FIG that we didn't know where you were. Who else then?"

"Come on, sis," Alex urged. "We're almost home. Can't you walk and think at the same time? It's not that hard to do."

"Oh, how would you know?" Alice snapped. "It's not like *you* ever think."

Alistair almost laughed at Alex's wounded expression. If there was one thing that made him feel like he was nearly home, it was hearing his brother and sister argue.

"Don't worry," he said to Tibby Rose, who was staring at his bickering siblings anxiously. "They're always like this. It's normal."

"Oh no!" said Alice suddenly.

"What's wrong?" said Tibby Rose.

"It couldn't be."

"What is it?" said Alistair.

"But I think it is!"

"Spit it out, sis," demanded Alex rudely.

"Mrs. Zetland!"

"Mrs. Zetland what?" said Alistair, noticing that Alex's white fur looked ghostlike in the moonlight.

"Oh no," said Alex.

Alistair sighed. "Would you two stop 'Oh no'ing' and just tell me what you're going on about?"

"Okay," said Alice. "But you're not going to like it."

"Especially since you're Mrs. Zetland's pet," Alex said.

"Though maybe that was all part of her act," said Alice.

"Good point." Alex nodded.

Alistair was starting to feel extremely frustrated with his brother and sister. "Just tell me," he demanded through gritted teeth.

"Mrs. Zetland is a spy," said Alice simply.

"What?" Alistair looked at his sister in amazement. "What are you talking about?"

"Who's Mrs. Zetland?" asked Tibby Rose.

"She's our downstairs neighbor," Alex explained. "And she makes really good biscuits."

"The morning we left to find you," Alice said to Alistair, "we met her on the stairs and she asked us where we were going, and why you weren't with us. We didn't want to tell her the truth, so we said that we were on our way to Stubbins and you'd gone on ahead of us. She was the only person we spoke to—it must have been her who told Horace and Sophia that they should follow us there to find you. And she must be the reason why they knew so much about us."

It was a more somber group who resumed the journey to Smiggins. Still, when he saw the first houses of his hometown in the pale light of dawn, it was all Alistair could do not to break into a run; he no longer felt his aching feet and tired legs.

But as they drew close to their apartment house, Alistair's high spirits were momentarily dampened. He'd known that Smiggins was no longer safe, that danger was close—but he hadn't realized that danger lived in the flat downstairs. It was a timely reminder that the life he once knew had changed irrevocably, and he felt a twinge of sadness as he and Tibby Rose tiptoed behind Alex and Alice past Mrs. Zetland's door on the way up the stairs to his aunt and uncle's apartment.

Alice knocked on the door so lightly that Alistair was sure his aunt and uncle—who were still asleep, no doubt—couldn't possibly hear it. But the door was flung open almost immediately.

As Uncle Ebenezer opened his mouth to exclaim, Alistair and the others hastily made shushing noises. Ebenezer accepted the need for silence without question, and stood aside to let them rush in, then quickly but soundlessly closed the door behind them.

"Alex, Alice—and Alistair!" Ebenezer cried as he surveyed the four mice standing before him. "Dear . . . purple? . . . Alistair!" His eyes shone with tears and Alistair found that he was so overcome with emotion at the sight of his uncle that he couldn't speak. He threw his arms around Ebenezer's portly body and squeezed.

Beezer, meanwhile, had appeared from the bedroom, yawning and beaming. "Oh, my dears!" She hugged Alice and Alex in turn, kissed the part of Alistair's head that wasn't buried in Uncle Ebenezer's squashy belly, and then turned to Tibby Rose with a friendly smile. "I don't believe we've been introduced," she said.

Alistair pulled away from his uncle's belly and announced, "This is my friend Tibby Rose. From Templeton—in Souris."

"Alistair fell on me," Tibby supplied helpfully.

"Tibby Rose from Templeton, eh?" Ebenezer looked thoughtful. He took Tibby's hand and shook it vigorously. "It's a great pleasure to meet you, my dear. A very great pleasure."

Alistair looked around the familiar room. More than once on the perilous journey home he had wondered if he would ever see this room again; he couldn't believe he was actually here.

"Have you been walking all night?" said Beezer, with a glance at the clock on the mantelpiece. "You must be exhausted. But what are you doing here, Alistair? When your uncle went to speak to his FIG contacts they told him that you'd been taken to a safe house far away." She turned to fix Alex and Alice with a stern look. "Which you two would have found out if you'd stayed here like you were supposed to!" Despite her scolding, Alistair could tell that she was so pleased to have them all safely home that she wasn't really angry at his brother and sister.

"But Alistair didn't stay at the safe house," Alex argued. "He and Tibby Rose traveled all the way home from Souris. So it was lucky we went to rescue them."

"Actually, it was lucky that *they* rescued *us*, Alex," Alice pointed out.

"It sounds like you all have a lot of explaining to do," Aunt Beezer remarked.

"And a lot of eating to do by the looks of you," added her husband. "You're all looking terribly thin. You must be hungry!"

"Am I ever!" said Alex, and he was off to the kitchen, his uncle close behind saying happily, "I'll make you the best breakfast you've ever had."

"Are you sure you have enough food?" Alistair heard Alex say in a muffled voice, as if his head was deep in the pantry.

"I hope so," said his uncle, his voice sounding slightly choked up. "But I've only been cooking for two this last week, haven't I?"

Despite Alex's fears the cupboard proved far from bare, and breakfast was a feast of eggs (poached, scrambled, coddled, hard boiled, soft boiled, and sunny-side-up), toast with jam (apricot, strawberry, blackberry—"No thanks," chorused Alistair and Tibby Rose—blueberry and raspberry) and crumpets with marmalade (orange, lime, and kumquat), pancakes (soaked in maple syrup), French toast (also soaked in maple syrup), porridge, cereal, and fresh fruit.

It was some time before the triplets and Tibby Rose were ready to recount their adventures, and once they began, it took them even more time (right through lunch, in fact) to tell everything that had happened. Aunt Beezer and Uncle Ebenezer looked grave and gloomy through most of their tellings—especially when Alice explained their suspicions about Mrs. Zetland. But there was one part of Alistair's story that brought smiles to the faces of his aunt and uncle.

"Zanzibar is free?" Ebenezer's face lit up and his mustache sprang up in delight. "Oh, happy day!" He leaned across the table and gave Beezer's hand a squeeze.

"I thought you hated FIG and Gerander, Uncle," Alice said.

"Ah well..." Ebenezer looked contrite. "I was angry and grief-stricken, and I was desperate to protect you kids. I thought if I ignored Gerander and FIG you would be safe, but I discovered it wasn't that simple. And I ignored my own principles." He shook his head in shame. "You remember what I told you? All that is necessary for evil to triumph is for good mice to do nothing. I've always believed that. So Beezer and I have decided we can no longer be content to do nothing. We have rejoined FIG."

"Hurrah!" said Alistair. "We want to join FIG too. Though I think Slippers Pink and Feast Thompson must be pretty mad at me and Tibby."

"You met Slippers Pink and Feast Thompson?" Alistair's uncle looked impressed.

"Do you know them, Uncle?"

"Me? No. I've heard of them, of course—they're very high up in FIG, very high indeed—but I've never met them personally. Your parents have, of course. Before they . . ." He trailed off into silence.

"Slippers Pink was happy about Zanzibar's escape too," Alistair remarked, resuming his story. "After we met the mouse from Gerander we were picked up by an owl, Oswald—the same owl who carried me from here to Templeton—and he took us to meet Slippers and Feast . . ."

But the news of Zanzibar's escape from the prison in the Cranken Alps was a rare piece of good news in Alistair's tale.

"So for all we know, Sophia and Horace could be on their way here now," Beezer summed up. "Fortunately, they don't know we've got Alistair here. Did they mention Tibby Rose at all?"

Alex and Alice looked at each other then shrugged.

"Not a word," said Alice. "Why should they?"

"Why indeed?" Ebenezer mused, stroking his mustache. "I don't suppose they knew where she was. No one did, after all. . . ."

Tibby looked at Alistair with raised eyebrows then said to the triplets' uncle, "Do you know me?"

"Know you?" Ebenezer looked startled. "Of course not. We've never met before today."

"But the way you were talking," Tibby persisted. "It sounded like maybe you'd heard of me before. Did you—did you know my father, perhaps?"

"Your father?" Ebenezer was looking uncomfortable.

"No, my dear," Beezer broke in. Her voice was kind but firm. "I'm afraid not. I think Ebenezer was just surprised that Alistair should be taken all the way to your house in Souris. Anyway, the important question is: What do we do now? Ebenezer and I will talk over everything you've told us, and then we'll all discuss it together over dinner."

That afternoon, Tibby Rose and the triplets took turns in the bathroom. Alistair enjoyed a good long shower with a lot of soap and scrubbing, after which his fur looked decidedly more ginger than purple. Then they had long naps, luxuriating in proper beds with clean sheets, Alice sharing her bed with Tibby Rose.

It was a clean and rested Alistair who was setting the table for dinner when he heard a tapping at the shutters. The sound gave him such a start that he dropped the cutlery with a clatter.

His uncle glanced at him quickly, then cautiously unlatched the window, pushed open the shutter, and peered out.

Hovering outside was a very grumpy-looking owl.

"Oswald!" said Alistair guiltily as Oswald fixed him with an ill-tempered glare and then settled on the windowsill.

"So you're here, are you? I suppose you thought you were clever running off on me like that. Well, I know a couple of mice who'll be having a very sharp word with you. Poor Slippers was beside herself with worry when I went back and told her what you'd done. Hmph." He turned his gaze to Alistair's uncle, said, "she sent you this," and dropped a note into Ebenezer's hand. He had just raised his huge wings to take off when Tibby Rose, who had been sitting on the couch with Alistair's copy of *Treasure Island*, jumped up and said, "Wait!"

The big bird paused.

"Oswald," said Tibby tentatively, "I'm really sorry we made things difficult for you, and I know you're pretty mad at us, but I was wondering if I could ask a favor."

"A favor?" snorted the owl. "You'd be lucky." Then, perhaps moved by the crushed look on Tibby's face, he said gruffly, "All right, what is it?"

"I was wondering if you would take a message to

Grandpa Nelson and Great-Aunt Harriet? I'd like to let them know that I'm okay."

The owl regarded her solemnly from under his great feathery brow and then sighed. "I suppose I owe them a message after swallowing the last one. But be quick about writing it, I haven't got all night."

Tibby Rose beamed. "Thank you, Oswald!"

Uncle Ebenezer fetched her a pen and a piece of paper, and Tibby Rose hurriedly wrote a message and then folded the paper. "And please tell Slippers Pink and Feast Thompson how sorry we are that we didn't wait for you like we'd agreed," she added as she slipped the message into the owl's beak.

Oswald gave an impatient cluck, then flapped his wings once, twice, and soared off the windowsill into the night.

Ebenezer gazed after the giant bird with a somewhat dazed expression. "Friendly chap, isn't he?"

It was Beezer, who had come in from the kitchen at the sound of Oswald's voice, who asked, "What does it say?," prompting her husband to remember the note in his hand.

Alistair's uncle hastily unfolded the piece of paper he was clutching and read aloud:

"*Dear Ebenezer and Beezer, I hardly know how to tell you this, but we have just heard the wonderful news that Rebus and*

Emmeline are alive! Alive? They're alive?!"

Beezer threw her arms around her husband's neck while their nephews and niece stood open-mouthed in shock. Alistair's heart began to race. Could it be true? But how . . . ? Where . . . ?

"Keep reading!" he urged his uncle.

"*They are in prison in Gerander—most probably on Atticus Island—where they have been held for some years.* Oh!"

Alistair's insides froze as Ebenezer's shoulders slumped. The hand holding the letter dropped to his side, and his other hand rose to cover his face. "Oh, my poor brother . . . ," he whispered. "And dear Emmeline . . . "

He resumed his perusal of the letter: "*Rest assured, every effort will be made to free them. . . .* " He read silently for a moment, his brow furrowed, then said, "Here's a bit about you, Alistair: *I am distressed to tell you that Alistair left the safe house. We encountered him briefly in Souris, along with a mouse called Tibby Rose, and his intention was to return to you. We are so worried about the pair of them. Please send us word with Oswald if you have heard from him. . . .* You know I am glad to see you, Alistair, but you really shouldn't have run off on Slippers Pink and Feast Thompson like that. Oh, what am I saying? I'm so glad to see you I don't care who you disobeyed! *You must leave Smiggins immediately . . .* Ah yes, it's as we thought. *As you are probably aware, much has been happening in Gerander. A special FIG meeting is to be held in Stetson* . . . That's to the northwest, I believe, near the Gerandan border. *I suggest we rendezvous there.*"

Ebenezer looked at Beezer. "What do you think, Beez?"

"That settles it really," said his wife. "We can't stay here, so we'll all go to Stetson for the meeting. But I really think this lot could use a good rest. I propose we set off first thing tomorrow morning."

As their aunt and uncle talked, Alistair, Alex, and Alice stared at each other.

"They're alive," Alice said finally, her eyes shining.

Alistair nodded wordlessly. So many emotions were crowding his mind he didn't know what to feel. Joy that Rebus and Emmeline were alive, of course. To think that he would see them again; feel his mother's gentle touch, hear his father's deep laugh. He felt weak suddenly, as a great weight of sadness that he had carried within him for four years began to dissolve. But then he remembered the tortured look in Uncle Silas's eyes as he'd spoken of his years imprisoned on Atticus Island. What must his parents have suffered? He gripped the ends of his scarf. Then he felt his brother's hand squeeze his shoulder.

"The FIG meeting . . . It's near Gerander," said Alex eagerly. "We'll be able to help look for them. You too, Tibby."

Alistair shot his brother a grateful look as Tibby, who had been standing a little apart, took a step forward, smiling. Privately, Alistair was a bit worried that Slippers Pink and Feast Thompson would not want him and Tibby Rose in FIG after their deception on the cliffs near Sadiz. Two of the highest-ranking members of FIG probably thought they were untrustworthy! But maybe if he sang them his mother's song they would relent? If it was related to the secret paths through Gerander that Slippers had spoken of, surely his information was too valuable to ignore, even if they were mad at him. It might even—Alistair felt a prick of excitement between his shoulder blades—it might even help in the rescue of his parents.

Over the family's favorite dinner of cheese and boiled potatoes, they celebrated the happy news that Emmeline and Rebus were alive.

"I knew it all along," Uncle Ebenezer kept saying. "Haven't I always told you how strong and courageous your father is?"

When they'd finished dinner, they turned to a discussion of the preparations they would need to make the following morning, with Tibby listing the ideal equipment for a proper survival kit.

Uncle Ebenezer pointed out that they would need to pack for winter, too, as there was no telling how long they would be away from home. "Your poor old scarf is looking a fright," he said to Alistair. "Imagine if your mother saw it looking like that! I'll wash it tonight, and it will be dry by morning."

Reluctantly, Alistair unwound the scarf from around his neck and held it out. As it unfurled, and he gazed at the familiar jumble of shapes and squiggles, and the long blue stripe down the center, the words of the old Gerandan suddenly came back to him. "A thin ribbon of land . . . ," he'd said. And that stripe of blue . . .

"Uncle Ebenezer, where is the River Winns?"

"The Winns?" His uncle looked surprised. "Ah, you're thinking about Timmy, are you? He certainly sounds like a character. You know, he reminds me a bit of—," Ebenezer broke off and shook his head. "No, that would be impossible. . . . " Then, catching sight of Alistair's questioning look, he said, "The Winns is Gerander's greatest river. It runs right down the center of the country, with hundreds of tributaries running off it. It's largely thanks to the Winns that Gerander is such a fertile, productive land."

So he was right, Alistair thought. The Winns was in Gerander. And it ran right through the center of the country, just like the blue stripe on his scarf ran right down the center. What was it Timmy had said? *It is the spine that knits our head to our feet.* Had the midnight blue mouse been looking at Alistair's scarf when he described the river as knitting the country together? Now that he thought about it, it seemed to Alistair that he had. As his uncle took the scarf and headed to the laundry, Alistair remembered what Slippers had said about the secret paths of Gerander. *They have never been recorded in writing,* she had told them, *but are passed down through families in other ways; they are sung or painted or danced.* Was it possible that instead of painting the paths, Emmeline had *knitted* them into his scarf? And that the scarf and the song went together? This was important news for Slippers Pink and Feast Thompson!

Alistair was trying to catch the eye of Tibby Rose, who was helping Aunt Beezer and Alex gather together the empty plates, when his uncle came back into the room and his aunt said, "Now let's talk of happier things and try to have a pleasant evening. We don't know what kinds of dangers and discomforts we might have ahead of us."

"I don't think anything could be more uncomfortable than rolling down a mountain in a barrel," said Alice.

"Or more dangerous than jumping off that cliff near Shambles," said Alex. "Did we tell you how high it was, Uncle? I bet the cliff you jumped from with the cheddar wasn't nearly so high."

"Well, it does sound like you were very brave,"

said their uncle. "But of course you forget that when I jumped off the cliff I was holding your father by the tail." Ebenezer indicated the couch. "Now imagine that the top of the couch is the cliff. . . . "

"Alistair?" called Alice a little while later. "Come over here and let me hold your tail."

Alistair looked over. His sister was standing on top of the couch next to Tibby Rose. Uncle Ebenezer was standing beside Tibby Rose, explaining something to her that involved lots of hand gestures and wiggles of the mustache. Tibby was straining slightly to bear the weight of Alex, who she was holding by the tail.

"Alistair," said Alice impatiently. "Hurry up!"

With a happy sigh, Alistair slipped off his chair and went over to join them. He was not going to let Alice hold him by the tail, but from now on he would join in any other adventure she and his brother had in mind.

"Coming," he said.

Acknowledgments

For insight, encouragement, and inspiration, I would like to thank David Francis, Belinda Bolliger, Barbara Mobbs, Helen Glad, and Lydia Papandrea.

Look out for the next book in the exciting
The Song of the Winns series in 2013, *The Spies of Gerander!*

⁓

A listair, come back!" called his uncle as Alistair stood in the middle of the road.

A giant owl swooped towards the ground, its talons outstretched. Alistair could just make out the shape of a mouse grasped in each talon.

"Oswald!" said Alistair, waving. "Over here."

The owl hovered inches above the ground, then carefully released its two passengers, who stumbled a moment before regaining their balance. In the twilight Alistair saw a tall lean mouse and a small slim one in shiny black boots. It was Feast Thompson and Slippers Pink.

"We'll walk from here," the slim mouse was telling the owl, "and meet up again later."

"Hi, Feast!" Alistair said as the owl soared into the darkening sky. "Hello, Slippers."

Feast Thompson and Slippers Pink turned at the sound of his voice. Slippers, Alistair noticed, was looking distinctly queasy; she hated flying.

"Alistair! Tibby Rose!" Slippers rushed over and hugged first Alistair and then Tibby Rose, who had joined him.

By this time, the others had left the shelter of the bushes, and Alistair introduced Slippers Pink and Feast Thompson to his family.

"A pleasure to meet two of FIG's highest operatives," said Ebenezer.

"People only call us that because we spend so much time in the air," said Slippers, laughing.

The group continued up the road together. Slippers Pink, walking with Beezer, led the way, followed by Ebenezer and Feast Thompson.

"It's just around the next bend," Slippers was saying. "FIG has taken over the Stetson school for our headquarters while everyone's away for the summer. The principal is a supporter."

"And when summer's over?" Beezer asked. "Where will the headquarters be then?"

Slippers shrugged her slim shoulders. "On the move again, I suppose. Setting up camp in a cave in a remote valley for a month or two, if we're lucky. More often it's just a week or so in a forest clearing or in the scrub along a deserted stretch of coast. It's been wonderful having a real base for a while: proper beds and running water and a cafeteria. Of course, we're keeping a low profile; I doubt anyone in the village even suspects that there's anyone staying at the school."

Alex, who was walking with Alice in front of Alistair

and Tibby Rose, groaned. "We're going to be hanging out at a school? Eating in the cafeteria?" Then he let out an *ooph* as Alice nudged him sharply in the ribs. "Hey, what did you do that for?" he demanded.

Alice hissed, "Because Feast Thompson and Slippers Pink have more important things to worry about than what the food is—"

But before she could finish her sentence they heard Feast Thompson say loudly, "I hope Tobias has found a good chef. Slippers and I have been traveling nonstop for the last couple of weeks, and I'd give anything to sit down to a big, hearty meal."

Alex didn't say anything, but Alistair saw him shoot a self-righteous look at Alice.

"Here's the turnoff," Slippers said, and at a fork in the road they turned left onto a narrow road winding up through an avenue of pine trees. "The school isn't actually in Stetson itself; it's on a hill above the town. It's great for security, because there's only one road in."

"Except if you arrive by owl," Feast pointed out.

After about ten minutes' walking, Alistair saw that up ahead the narrow road opened out onto a large flat plateau partially enclosed by a wall of rock. He could just make out clusters of dark shapes, which must be the school buildings. As they drew close two mice stepped out onto the road to block their way.

Slippers Pink and Feast Thompson moved forward.

"Hi, Flora," said Slippers to the tall blonde mouse. She turned to the tall brown one. "Is that you, Maxwell? It's been ages."

"I've been undercover the last few months," the brown mouse said briefly. Alistair noticed that Slippers and Feast nodded but didn't ask any questions about where Maxwell had been or why.

"Who else have you got there?" Flora wanted to know, peering past Slippers and Feast to where Alistair and the others were standing a few feet away.

"We've got Ebenezer and Beezer from Smiggins, and their niece and nephews and a friend."

Max consulted a list, then said, "So that's Alex, Alice, Alistair, and Tibby Rose, right?" He checked off their names and said, "We've been expecting you."

Flora told Beezer and Ebenezer, "You can have adjoining rooms in the dormitory building for the next couple of nights. After that..." She shrugged. "We've just had word from one of our patrols that they've found a group of refugee families from Gerander hiding near the border. They'll be here within forty-eight hours, and it sounds like they might have been injured in the escape. We'll probably have to move you so they can have your rooms. You can bed down in the hall after that; plenty are."

"Of course," Ebenezer murmured. His expression had grown concerned at the mention of injured mice.

Flora continued, "You're in room 17. The dorm is in block 1, on the other side of the oval. I'd suggest you drop off your bags and then go straight to the hall, which is the building beside it. Tobias is going to say a few words before dinner." She indicated a building close by; its high windows were lit up. "That's the cafeteria there."

"Thank you," said Beezer. "Come on, everyone." She and Ebenezer began to lead the way across the grassy oval.

"What about Slippers and Feast?" Alistair said, hesitating. He couldn't wait to tell Slippers Pink and Feast Thompson the secret he'd discovered about his scarf, but he knew he had to wait until they were alone. When Slippers Pink had told them about the hidden paths through Gerander, she had made Alistair and Tibby Rose promise that they would never reveal the secret to anyone.

The tall dark brown mouse and smaller almond mouse exchanged a wry look. "If I know Tobias," said Slippers, "we probably won't be staying long."

Frances Watts worked as an editor for ten years before writing her bestselling picture book *Kisses for Daddy*, illustrated by David Legge. Other books include the award-winning *Parsley Rabbit's Book about Books*, *Captain Crabclaw's Crew* (both illustrated by David Legge), and *A Rat in a Stripy Sock*, illustrated by David Francis. As well as continuing to write picture books, Frances has written a series of chapter books about two unlikely superheroes, Extraordinary Ernie and Marvellous Maud, illustrated by Judy Watson. *The Secret of the Ginger Mice* is the first book in The Song of the Winns series. Frances lives in Sydney and divides her time between writing and editing.

www.franceswatts.com